Irish Legends

MARGARET SIMPSON

Illustrated by **Michael Tickner**

Scholastic Children's Books,
Commonwealth House, 1-19 New Oxford Street,
London WC1A 1NU

A division of Scholastic Limited
London - New York - Toronto - Sydney - Auckland
Mexico City ~ New Delhi ~ Hong Kong

Published in the UK by Scholastic Ltd, 2000

ISBN 0 590 54377 6

Typeset by Falcon Oast Graphic Art, East Hoathly, East Sussex.
Printed by Cox & Wyman, Reading, Berks.

2 4 6 8 10 9 7 5 3 1

Contents

Introduction

The stories in this book were first told hundreds, maybe even thousands of years ago. The people who told them – and the people who listened – were Celts. The Celts have been called the first masters of Europe. They were awesome warriors, great farmers and traders, and fantastic metalworkers. They loved bright clothes and jewellery. And best of all, they loved a really good yarn. In fact, storytellers, bards, and poets were as important as kings in old Ireland. This wasn't just because they entertained people. It was also because stories made people famous and meant that even after they were dead their names lived on. The stories are important to us too, because through them we can see the people of old Ireland, and understand what they believed about the world, and about themselves.

So, welcome to the world of Irish Legend – a world of warriors and magic, where nothing is ever as it seems. Visit the mysterious Otherworld. Meet magicians, ghosts and gods. Follow them as they change shape and cast spells. Will you ever come back? We'll see.

Some of these Irish stories are much older than others. Here the oldest tales are told first, and the youngest last – but even the youngest story has been told over and over again for at least 1500 years!

Legend 1: The man with the silver arm

A lot of the old Irish stories are about war and fighting. This is because the history of old Ireland is all about invasions. Wave after wave of people moved northwards across Europe from Scythia, Galatia and Greece, starting maybe as early as 2500 BC – and each group of new arrivals fought the last.

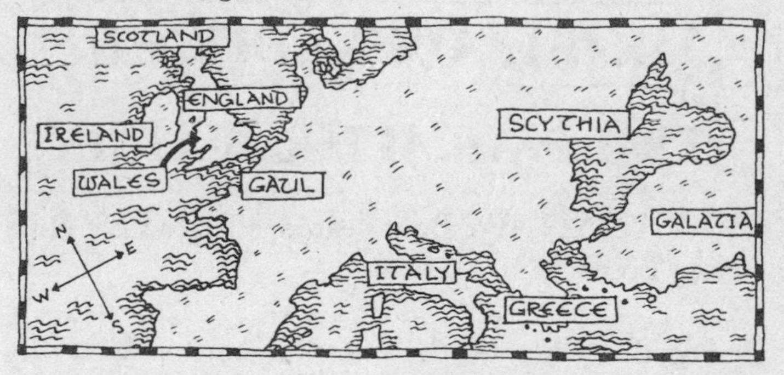

Top Ten Legend number one comes from the time of the fourth invasion. All you need to know to start with is that the Tuatha De Danaan were the good guys, and that the Formorians and the Fir Bolg were the bad guys.

Of course, in those days, there were no newspapers,

but if there had been, this is how the story of Nuada Silver Arm might have been reported around 300 BC. They didn't use the calendar we do today, so the dates are given in terms of the four most important festivals of the Celtic Year – *Samhain*, 1st November; *Imbolc*, 1st February; *Beltain*, 1st May; and *Lughnasa*, 1st August.

THE GREAT MEDICAL BREAKTHROUGH

TWO DAYS AFTER BELTAIN

TAKE THAT! •Fir Bolg beaten •Tuatha De Rule •King Loses Arm

Today the King of the wicked Fir Bolg lay dead on the battlefield of Moytura among the bodies of thousands of warriors killed in the terrible battle. With him died the hopes of the Fir Bolg. Now there can be no more argument. The great Tuatha De Danaan are the rulers of Ireland.

EVIL KING BREATHES HIS LAST ON BATTLEFIELD DEATH BED

Brave King Nuada led his men to victory – but he paid a high price.

His right arm was hacked off in the battle.

YOU WIN SOME YOU LOSE SOME

"Nuada has lost a lot of blood and is very weak," said spokesman, Ogma. "God-Doc Diancecht★ is treating him and we hope he will live to fight another day."

But everyone knows that with only one arm, Nuada can no longer rule Ireland.

Even though he won a great victory, he must stand aside for another leader.

The severed arm was wrapped in moss and buried deep under the battlefield so it could not be eaten by crows.

LOST LIMB LIES LOW!

★ Dee'an kecht. He was the god of healing.

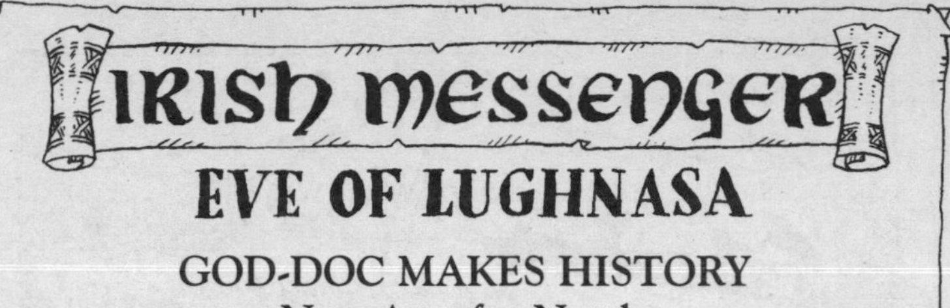

EVE OF LUGHNASA

GOD-DOC MAKES HISTORY

New Arm for Nuada

Three months after the battle of Moytura, God-Doc Diancecht has made medical history. He has fitted ex-king Nuada with a silver arm.

"The arm has been ready since a week after the battle," said God-Doc D. "I couldn't fit it sooner because we were waiting for the stump of Nuada's arm to heal."

At a press conference, he showed journalists a working model of the arm and hand. It has an elbow that bends and fingers that grip.

SOLID GOLD?! DID IT COST AN ARM AND A LEG?!!

Designed by Credne, the god of metalwork, it was cast in solid silver by Giobniu, the divine blacksmith.

"With this, Nuada will be as good as new," said the delighted doc. "Now there is no reason for him not to be king."

NUADA IS FULLY ARMED AGAIN!

The warlords who once swore allegiance to Nuada disagreed.

"The laws of the Tuatha De say that a king must be whole and without blemish," said one. "You can't tell me that a man with a false arm is whole – even if the arm is made of solid silver."

Others said they felt the silver arm was unnatural. One man said that he thought it would cause war again in Ireland if Nuada laid claim to the throne. "Bres the Handsome is our leader now. He's making a good job of it," he said.

It seems brave Nuada agreed with him. Friends said that he didn't care about being king, he was happy to be alive and to serve the country under Bres."

Yesterday Nuada was seen practising his sword strokes with his new arm.

A SHINING EXAMPLE OF SUPER-SWORDSMANSHIP!

FIVE YEARS LATER. . .

IRISH MESSENGER

TWENTY DAYS BEFORE SAMHAIN

"SHAPE UP OR SHIP OUT!"
Lords Warn Bres

Last week the warlords of the Tuatha De Danaan warned Bres: "If you want to stay king, stop favouring the Formorians!"

Ever since he was made king, Bres – whose father was a Formorian chief – has angered the Tuatha De with high taxes and hard work, while the wild Formorians get away with murder.

BRES.... FAIR OF FACE.... UNFAIR BY NATURE !!

At first the wily Bres pretended he didn't know what the Tuatha De were talking about. Then he said he would mend his ways – provided the lords allowed him to be king for another seven years.

Now it looks as if he's just playing for time. Bres has gone to visit One-Eyed Balor, Lord of the Isles and Indech, King of the Formorians.

BEAUTY MEETS BEAST!

Before leaving he said it was just a goodwill visit.

"Gone to raise an army, more like," said one of the Tuatha De who refused to be named.

"If only Nuada had not been maimed in battle, we wouldn't be in this mess," said another.

BRES HAS TRICK UP HIS SLEEVE . . . ALL BECAUSE THERE'S NO ARM IN NUADA'S ! ! !

40 DAYS AFTER IMBOLC

MIRACLE-MAN MIACH!

Nuada's arm dug up and sewn on

Lords of the Tuatha De could hardly believe their eyes today when Nuada Silver Arm appeared in public with his right arm as good as new.

"When I unwrapped it, it was a bit discoloured and soggy but I took it back to Nuada's house, washed it, and sewed it back on."

NUADA'S ARM IS RIGHT WHERE IT BELONGS!

At first they thought it must be a trick. Then Miach, 17-year-old son of God-Doc Diancecht, spoke up. He said that he had dug up Nuada's severed arm and found it had not rotted even though it is over six years since it was hacked off.

"It was still wrapped in moss," said Miach.

Critics – including his own father, God-Doc Diancecht – said it was impossible. They challenged him to explain how he had done it.

Miach was reluctant to give away his secrets, but finally explained that he had held it in place for nine days while chanting.

He refused to reveal the words he used, but it seems likely he used the old spell, "Let this be joined nerve to nerve, sinew to sinew, vein to vein, skin to skin." By the ninth day, said Miach, Nuada's arm was joined to his body and as good as new.

MIACH'S MYSTERIOUS SURGERY IS A RESOUNDING SUCCESS!!

As Miach finished speaking, a cry came from the crowd for Nuada to show the people his arm. He bared his right arm and whirled a heavy spear high above his head. There was not a scar to be seen.

Cheers went up, and then the shout, "Long live King Nuada!" Two warlords raised Nuada on their shoulders and carried him through cheering crowds. Soon everyone was calling for Nuada to lead the Tuatha De Danaan to victory against the evil Bres and the Formorian hordes.

Nuada clenched his two fists in triumph. He agreed to be their leader and ordered everyone to attend a great feast at Tara next week.

12 DAYS BEFORE BELTAIN

Miracle-boy murdered by Death-dealing God-Doc-Dad

Miach, the miracle boy, who last month restored the arm of King Nuada, has been stabbed to death by his angry father, Diancecht.

His sister Airmid found him bleeding to death with a sword sticking out of his skull.

"I tried to save his life, but it was no good," said Airmid. "This was my father's fourth attack on him. Miach had healed himself from the other three wounds, but this time the sword penetrated his brain. He died in my arms."

Asked why Diancecht had killed his son, Airmid explained that the old doc was jealous of his young son's skill.

"He couldn't bear it that Miach could fix Nuada's own arm back on when he couldn't," she said.

King Nuada was told the news. "I owe my kingdom to that young hero," he said. "Diancecht will be punished for this. And I will never forget what Miach did for me. I swear on my mended arm that I will not rest until the Tuatha De have won a great victory over the Formorians."

MIACH DIES IN SISTER'S ARMS FOLLOWING FATHER'S ATTACK OF JEALOUSY!!

15 DAYS AFTER BELTAIN

New Life from the Grave

This is a picture of the grave of Miach the Miracle Boy. Already, within days of his burial, it is covered with healing herbs.

MIACH MAKES MAGIC FROM BEYOND THE GRAVE!

The shoots came sprouting through the earth the very next day after his body was buried. Now there are three hundred and sixty-five different herbs – one for every joint and sinew in the human body. Each one is a fine healthy plant.

His sister Airmid was at the grave today, picking and sorting the herbs.

"Miach has sent these herbs to heal every ailment known to man woman or child," she said. "From now on there will be no illness we cannot cure."

IRISH MESSENGER

WRECKED!!

Mad God-Doc Strikes Again

16 DAYS AFTER BELTAIN

All the herbs sorted by Airmid have been uprooted from Miach's grave. They were found trampled and scattered by Airmid when she arrived at the grave to continue her task this morning.

Doc Diancecht has been in hiding since his son's death, but a woman who lives near by said she had seen a man leaving the grave yesterday evening at dusk. "I've seen Doc Diancecht once or twice, and there's no doubt in my mind it was him," said mother of thirteen, Eithne Mac Moran (32).

A former friend said of the doc, who did not want to be named, "He is mad with envy. He just can't bear his son's success."

Airmid is said to be in despair – now no one knows which herb does what. Miach's gift to humanity has been destroyed.

SAD SISTER SEES RESULTS OF DASTARDLY DAD'S HORRIBLE HANDYWORK !!

FIVE DAYS AFTER LUGHNASA

GOTCHA!

One-Eyed Balor has the spear of Lugh Long-Arm sticking out of his eye. Lugh is the brilliant young hero who fought beside King Nuada to conquer the Formorians and the wicked Fir Bolg.

BALOR GETS AN EYEFUL!!

Now the Tuatha De Danaan are rulers of the whole of Ireland.

There were many great heroes in this last campaign. Young men who gave their lives for the future of the Race of Danaan.

But as we remember the fallen, let's not forget young Miach, who rejoined the arm of King Nuada, and was killed by his father for his pains.

Without Nuada, there would have been no victory.

Without Miach, no King Nuada.

Top Facts 1: Become an instant Irish expert!

In order to understand the Irish legends, you need to get up to speed on Irish history – or what passes for Irish history as there's a lot of myth and legend thrown in. Here's a quick potted history to make YOU an INSTANT EXPERT!

Who were the Irish, anyway?

The Irish – or most of them – were Celts. And the Celts at one stage ruled the whole of Europe. That includes Ireland.

So if the Irish were Celts, who are all these other groups then?

The Celts were just one among a number of tribes. That basically means people connected to each other by birth or marriage and their servants and hangers-on. After a few generations this would be quite a lot of people.

So the Tuatha whatsit were one of these tribes, were they?

That's right. In fact, their name actually means Danu's

Tribe. They were the fourth lot of people who invaded Ireland. They claimed to be descended from the goddess Danu. They came from northern Greece, and they were the best storytellers. Many of the top ten stories were first told by the Tuatha De.

And the Formorians?

Well, the Tuatha De called them nasty, hairy unco-operative, uncivilized demons. So this probably means they were the original native population of Ireland, who didn't much like invaders. They're the only ones who may not have been Celts.

What about the Fir Bolg?

Oh them. They were the third wave of invaders, who were pushed out, killed, or turned into slaves by the Tuatha De. They too had come from Greece, but hundreds of years before, in boats made of skins called coracles. They fought the Formorians, and divided Ireland into five provinces which still exist today.

When the Tuatha De arrived, the Fir Bolg king, One-Eyed Balor, escaped to the Western Isles of Scotland, where he waited his chance to come back and drive out the Tuatha De.

So if the Fir Bolg were the third wave of invaders and the Tuatha De were the fourth, who were the other two?

The first lot followed a man called Partholon. They were all wiped out by a plague. Next came the Children of Nemed. They came from Greece and it wasn't long before they were driven back there again.

Is that the lot, then? Were the Tuatha De the last?
No. The last lot were the Sons of Mil. They were Gaels, another subgroup from Spain, and they conquered or drove out the Tuatha De. Their leader was called Amergin White-Knee, and he was a magician and a bard, or poet.

Was Amergin a real person?
Probably. There's a real poem that he's supposed to have written.

What about Nuada and Diancecht?
They may have been based on real people. They were Tuatha De heroes, so from the storyteller's point of view, that made them gods, along with Diancecht, Ogma, Credne, Giobniu. . .

All right, all right, I can't keep up. Let's stick to facts. When did all these invasions happen?

No one's too sure. The monks who wrote down the stories weren't too strong on dates. The invasions probably happened over a period of about eight hundred years (at least). Top Ten story number one ends right at the beginning of Christian times in Ireland, probably around AD 400. So working back from that, the earliest stories would date from 400 BC – though they are probably even older.

Legend 2: The curse of Macha

Number two in our Top Ten Irish Legends is the story of Macha – and it's part of a much longer tale called *The Cattle Raid of Cooley*, which was a long story or epic all about a war fought over a bull between Queen Maev of Connacht and King Conchobar of Ulster. Crunnchu Mac★ Agnoman was a rich farmer living in Ulster at that time. He was a widower, living with grown-up sons. Then one day, something very strange happened. Find out what through the letters his son Connor wrote to his younger brother Donal who was away on a long quest with the great Cuchulain.✪

★ The word "Mac" means "son of"; it occurs in a lot of early Irish surnames.
✪ Coo-hool'in

A FARMER GETS A WIFE.

Cold Ridge Farm,
Ulster.
16 days after Samhain

Dear Donal,

You'll never guess what's happened. The old man has got himself a new woman! She's a bit of all right too. To look at, I mean. Other than that I would say she was a bit strange.

What happened, I come in from milking the cows one day last week, and the place was warm. And clean. The fire was made up, and a fine smell of broth cooking, and this dame busying herself about the place as if she'd lived among us all her life.

"Hello," I said. "And who would you be?"

"My name is Macha," she said.

"Housekeeper, are you?" I said. Though even as I spoke I was thinking she didn't look like a housekeeper. Her dress was too fine. Good wool, I would say. She looked like a lady.

"We'll see," said this dame. "There's some water hot if you want to wash."

"Oh," I said, a bit taken aback. "We don't go much on washing in this house." Which is true, as you know, since Mammy died. But since the water was there, a big cauldron heating over the fire, I thought, why not? I took a bowl out in the yard – you weren't going to catch me washing in front of her. When I came back, there was a clean shirt waiting for me.

Well, I thought. I don't know what she meant by "We'll see." She knows how to keep house, all right. Last time I had a clean shirt laid out like that was when Mammy was alive.

Next thing I know, I hear the old man coming across the yard.

"Evening," he says, as he takes off his bonnet.

"Good evening, Crunnchu," says she.

"My, but that's a fine smell of broth," says he.

"Glad you like it, Crunnchu," says she.

So then she goes out for something, and he turns to me.

"Very nice," he says to me. "So where'd you find her?"

"Me?" I said. "I never found her. I thought it was a housekeeper you'd brought in."

"I never seen her before in my life," said he. "I came back here after milking this morning, and there she was, poking the fire. This afternoon, she wanted a couple of rabbits. When I last went out she was skinning them ready to cook."

"So who is she?" I asked.

"I don't know," said he. "But I don't care much. She can stay as long as she likes so far as I'm concerned."

She came back in then. I tell you, Donal, she's a fine-looking woman. Long black hair. Fine pale skin. Eyes grey as the sea. And good bones, like a thoroughbred horse. It's hard to put an age to her, but she's too young for the old feller, that's for sure. So I tossed my head at her and gave her a bit of a wink. She smiled at me, and then I caught the old man's eye on me.

"You'll be going away out after you've eaten," he said.

"No," said I. "It's a cold night. I thought I'd stay."

"You'll be going away out," said he, and narrowed his eyes the way he used to when you knew he was going to thrash you.

"Yes. Well, if that's the way it is," I said. I tried to catch Macha's eye again but she was turned away, busy with the pot, serving our meal.

It was a very good meal, an' all. I tell you, Donal, I've not eaten so well in that house these ten years since our Mammy died. Soon as we were finished, the old man was telling me to get away out. So I did. I went thinking, "Silly old buffer. Don't tell me he fancies his chances with her. She wouldn't look at him, not with his gammy leg and his neck like a stringy old fowl."

Well, just shows how wrong I was. When I came back, weren't they tucked up in bed together? Next morning she's making porridge, and he's looking like the cat who's licked the cream.

"Didn't think she'd want a soft boy like you, did you?" he said to me when we went out to the animals.

I felt like saying, "There must be something wrong with her, to want an old beggar like you."

But you know what he's like. He'd lay about me with that stick of his soon as look at me. I held my tongue.

All the best,

Your brother,

Connor

Cold Ridge Farm,
Ulster.
Four days before Beltain

Dear Donal,

That Macha I was telling you about, she's some runner. Not that you'd ever have known except that Jet, our new young stallion, broke loose last week. Old man started yelling it was my fault, told me to go after him. I looked at him as if he was mad. I thought, no way anyone's going to catch that stallion, not till he tires hisself out. Then doesn't Macha come flying out of

the house – she must have heard us arguing – and she was off after the horse like the wind. Over field and bush she went, her skirts hitched up, jumping ditches and all sorts. I couldn't believe my eyes when I saw the distance closing between her and that horse. Then they were both gone from view, and I thought, well she's a good runner, I'll give her that, but she'll never be able to keep it up.

Next thing, and the stallion's trotting nice as you like back into the yard, with Macha on his back. She'd caught him. I tell you there's not many women can do that.

All the best,

Connor

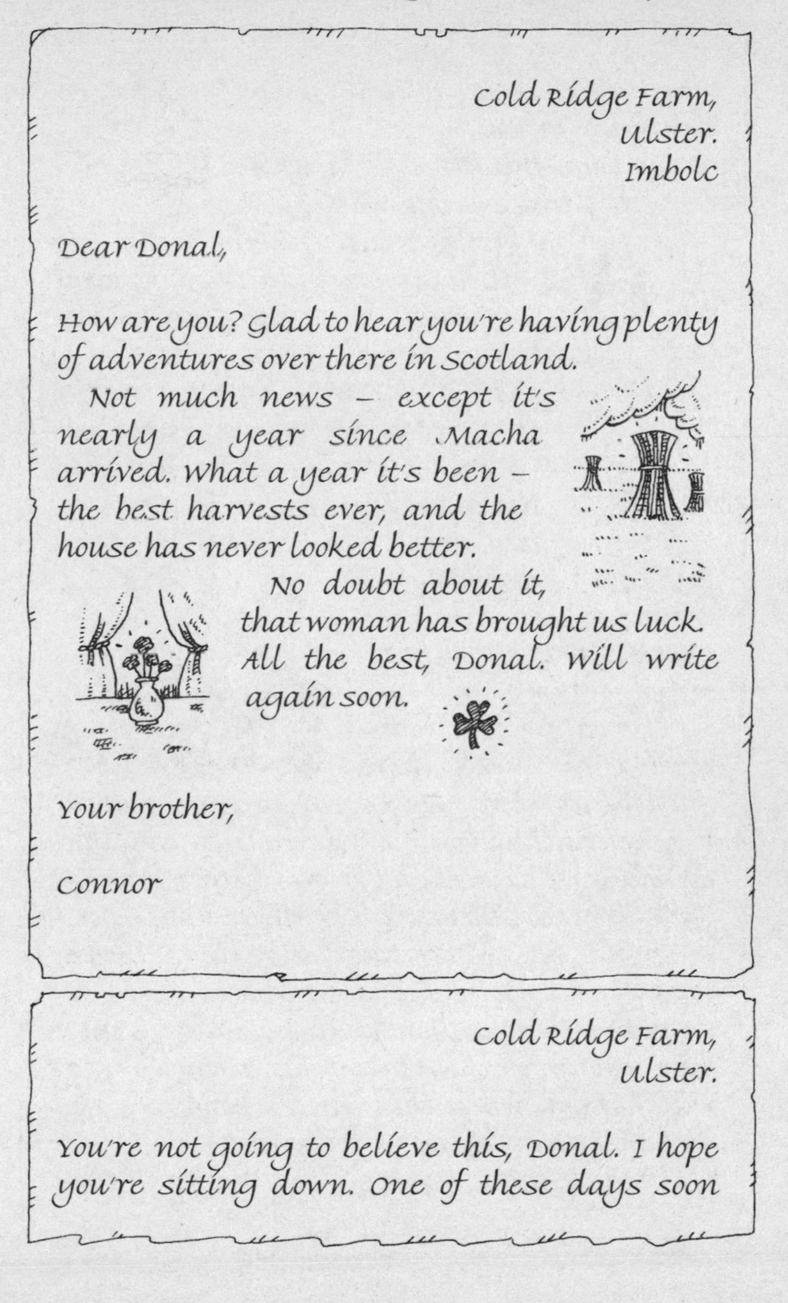

Cold Ridge Farm,
Ulster.
Imbolc

Dear Donal,

How are you? Glad to hear you're having plenty of adventures over there in Scotland.

Not much news – except it's nearly a year since Macha arrived. What a year it's been – the best harvests ever, and the house has never looked better.

No doubt about it, that woman has brought us luck. All the best, Donal. Will write again soon.

Your brother,

Connor

Cold Ridge Farm,
Ulster.

You're not going to believe this, Donal. I hope you're sitting down. One of these days soon

now, you're going to have a new brother or sister.

I've been thinking for a while that Macha was looking a bit thick around the waist. Well, it's more than thick around the waist now, she's enormous. Never seen a woman get so big so fast. If she was a cow, I would think it was twins she was having.

I'm not sent out of the house in the evenings any more. They sit either side of the fire, her and the old man, like they've been married twenty years. But the strange thing about it is, no one outside the house even knows she's there. She told us we're not to speak to anyone about her, neither him nor me. I don't know why that is, she won't say. I don't know whether it's that she's from the Otherworld, or whether she's got a husband somewhere that she doesn't want finding out where she is. So whatever you do, don't be telling anyone that our daddy's got a new fancywoman. Heaven alone knows what will happen when this child's born, cos you can't keep a child secret for long.

I heard them arguing for the first time

today. He wants to go to the great assembly at Lughnasa, and she doesn't want him to go.

"But sure and I have to go," he told her. "I have animals to sell."

"Are you sure it's not the mead and the horse-racing you're after?" says she.

"Well, and can a man not enjoy a glass of mead and a bet on the horses?" said he.

"It's what the mead will do to your tongue that worries me," said Macha. "I know what you men are like. You get a cup of mead inside you, and you'll be talking about me right left and centre."

"And what's wrong with that?" said the old man. "If I talk about you it's because I'm proud of you. Ye gods, anyone would be proud of a woman like you. You're a fantastic woman, Macha. And to think it's my baby you've got in there."

"I don't think you understand, Crunnchu," said Macha, and very serious she looked now. "It's a solemn geas★ I placed on you when I came here.

★ A geas is a sort of unbreakable promise.

You break it at your peril."

"Oh, I know, I know," said the old man. "I'm not one to break a geas. I'll keep my mouth tight shut and never say a word. They can all think I live on in a cold house with no woman in my bed. Doesn't matter to me, because I know better."

"But why do you have to go in the first place? The baby's due any time, I want you here."

"Now listen. Just because you can run like the wind, and you have me eating out of your hand, you needn't think you can boss me about altogether. Every year I go to that fair at Lughnasa. And no woman, not even you, is going to tell Crunnchu Mac Agnoman what to do."

She sulked that evening. He couldn't get another word out of her.

"This is going to end badly," is what she said to me.

I hope she's wrong. It's been like everything we touch turns to gold since she's been with us.

All the best, Donal. Write soon.

Your brother,

Connor

Cold Ridge Farm,
Ulster.
Five days after Lughnasa

Dear Donal.

Bad news.

Macha was right about the old man. He got well drunk at the fair, and you know how drink loosens his tongue. He was watching the races and King Conchobar and all his Druid priests and bards★ and courtiers were standing near by watching too. And the king's horses were doing pretty well, they were winning every race going. And people were cheering them on, saying there were no horses in the world to

★ Bards were Druid poets.

equal the king's, you know the sort of thing. The kind of thing folks always say to flatter the king.

Then doesn't the old man pipe up. At first I thought he was going to say something about the stallion, but no. Wasn't it Macha he started to boast about.

"Pah! My young wife Macha at home runs faster than them!" he shouts.

"A young wife? You, Crunnchu?" shouted one of the king's men. He laughed with some of his mates.

"Dream on Crunnchu," they shouted.

"I tell you I have," shouts my dad. "A beautiful woman she is, finer than any of your wives, I can tell you. A good strong woman! She cooks, she bakes, she washes. I tell you there's nothing that woman can't do."

"She even races faster than the king's horses," shouted one of the king's men.

"Aye, you laugh, but she does!" shouted my father, waving his stick in the air.

So now the king chimes in. "Who is this man?" he wants to know. "Tie him up! And go and get this famous wife of his. We'll see whether she can outrun my horses or not."

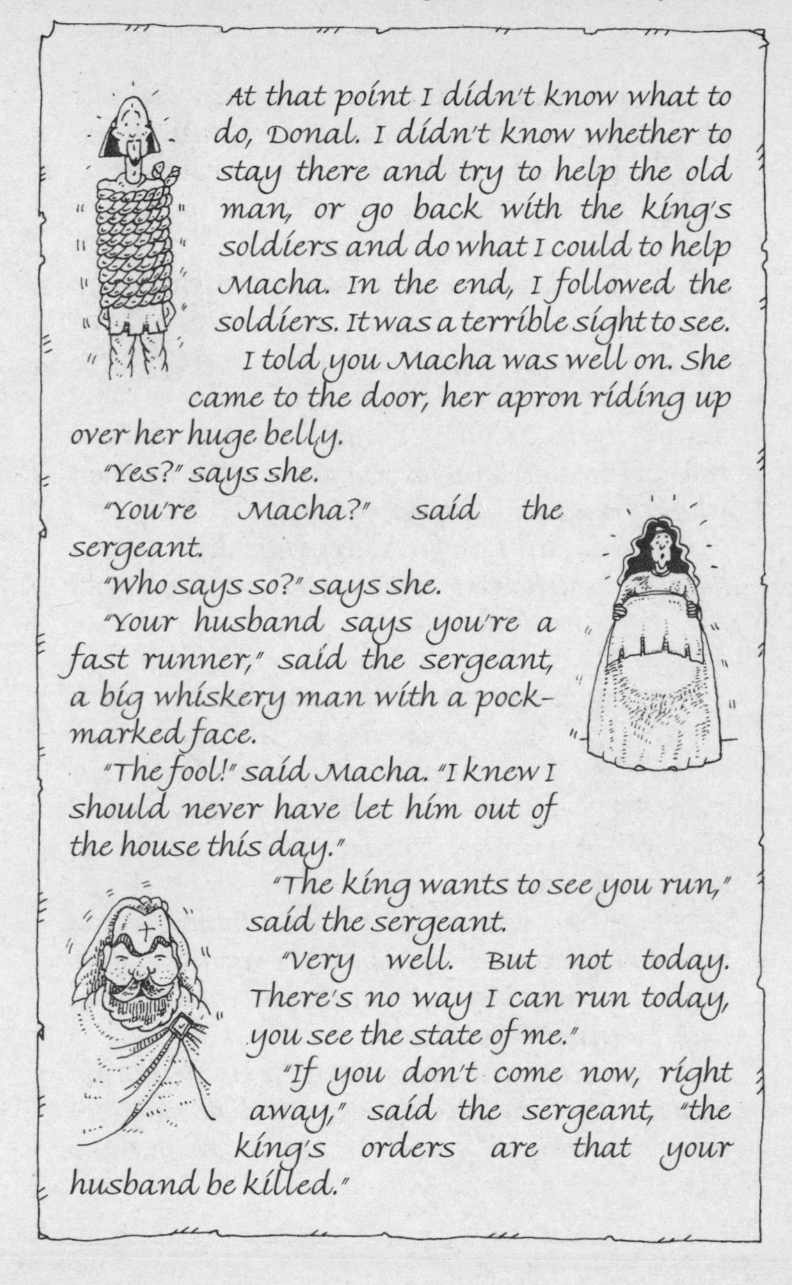

At that point I didn't know what to do, Donal. I didn't know whether to stay there and try to help the old man, or go back with the king's soldiers and do what I could to help Macha. In the end, I followed the soldiers. It was a terrible sight to see.

I told you Macha was well on. She came to the door, her apron riding up over her huge belly.

"Yes?" says she.

"You're Macha?" said the sergeant.

"Who says so?" says she.

"Your husband says you're a fast runner," said the sergeant, a big whiskery man with a pock-marked face.

"The fool!" said Macha. "I knew I should never have let him out of the house this day."

"The king wants to see you run," said the sergeant.

"Very well. But not today. There's no way I can run today, you see the state of me."

"If you don't come now, right away," said the sergeant, "the king's orders are that your husband be killed."

Macha went and got her shawl. The king's men dragged her along behind their horses. It wasn't a pretty sight, but I'll say this for her. She's got guts. When they shoved her before the king, she wasn't grovelling. She held her head high. Like a queen she was. Meanwhile the old man was ashen. He was sober enough now to know he'd broken his geas. And we both know what it means to do that, Donal.

"So what can I do for Your Majesty," Macha says to Conchobar. "Why have I been brought here like this?"

"Your husband boasts you can run faster than my horses," said King Conchobar. "I want to see." He had a smile on his face, as if he was enjoying the idea of seeing her make a fool of herself.

"You're going to ask me to run today?" said Macha. "Do you want to humiliate me? You see my belly. My time is due. I cannot run today."

"Very well," said Conchobar. He turned to his soldiers. "Unsheathe your swords!" he shouted. "Cut this stupid, ignorant, boastful man to pieces!"

"No!" screamed Macha. "How can you do this? My husband drank too much and he spoke too freely. Is that a reason for him to die? Show some mercy, by all the gods!"

"You can save him," said Conchobar. "All you have to do is run." It was so obvious, Donal, that he wanted to see her make a fool of herself.

"Very well," said Macha. "I will run. You can have your laugh at my expense. But know this. For your pitiless behaviour, you and all your men will suffer far greater shame than I do now."

"Who are you?" asked King Conchobar. I think for the first time he was beginning to think there might be more to Macha than met the eye.

"I am Macha, daughter of Sainreth Mac Imbaith. And I will run. Bring the horses level with me."

The horses were brought. My father couldn't bear to look, he was weeping with shame.

"Loose them!" called Macha.

The horses were off, and she after them. It was just like before, except this time she overtook them all, and raced like the wind to the winning post. And there she fell, Donal. She

was in labour, and crying out in pain. Before any of the horses had so much as reached her she gave birth to twins. And it was the weirdest thing, Donal. She was crying for help, but not a man amongst us could move a muscle. Then we heard her say.

"I curse you with this! From this day, the shame and disgrace which you have inflicted on me here will bring shame and disgrace on you all. When Ulster is in danger her men will become weak and helpless as a woman in labour. This curse will last for nine generations!"

With that she died. My father is heart-broken, and I think the king is scared, for it's a terrible curse. Already they're calling the place where the race was run by a new name: Emhain Macha – Macha's Twins.

Donal, I hope this curse doesn't extend to you or the great Cuchulain. Me, I'm so weak I can hardly lift my pen to write.

Write soon and tell me how you are.

Your brother,

Connor

Top Facts 2: Irish gods and goddesses

Was the mysterious Macha a goddess as the Tuatha De believed? Or is this a story about having to hide people from the "wrong" tribe – and about what happened when they got caught? Whatever *you* think, the Celts believed that Macha was a goddess – and a pretty scary one at that.

Here's a run-down on the Top Ten Irish gods and goddesses.

1 The Dagda was the massive father god of Ireland. His name means "The Good God". He was a rough, tough god who always wore his tunic up round his bum. He had an enormous club – one end of which killed the living while the other brought the dead back to life – and a huge cauldron from which he fed people.

When the Tuatha De Danaan were unready for war with the Formorians, they sent the Dagda to seek a truce. The Dagda liked porridge and the Formorians knew this. They made a huge cauldron of porridge and mixed into it whole goats, cows and sheep. Then they dug a pit and poured the porridge into it, threatening to kill the Dagda unless he ate up every drop. The Dagda seized a huge ladle and ate the lot. Afterwards he was so full that he could hardly walk. He leant on his enormous club as he walked away. The club made a deep track in the land, which formed a boundary dyke known forever after as the "track of Dagda's club".

2 Dana was the Mother of Them All. Well, not quite all. Danu was the mother of the Tuatha De Danaan. Dana was goddess of fertility, plenty, learning, and culture. Despite having been mother to a great tribe of heroes, she doesn't come into the stories much. Maybe this is because she was also known as. . .

3 **...Brigid**, goddess of poetry and learning, who was a daughter of the Dagda. She had two sisters, also called Brigid (which must have made it a bit confusing when dad called her name). One sister was a healer, and the other a silversmith. Brigid later became the Christian Saint Brigid, who was born at sunrise and fed from the milk of a magic cow. Saint Brigid kept a sacred fire going, surrounded by a high hedge. She and nineteen nuns took it in turns to guard this fire. No men were allowed in.

4 **The Morrigan** was absolutely terrifying. She was the goddess of war and battle. If you wanted to win a war, it was important to get her on your side. Before battle she was seen washing mangled limbs – the limbs of the men destined to die!

She had a yearly meeting with the Dagda at Samain (Hallowe'en); at one of these he persuaded her to abandon the Formorians and fight on the side of the Tuatha De. When the Tuatha De finally won their war against the Formorians, she sang the news of their victory from the hill-tops, telling the rivers, hills and valleys of the land itself that the Tuatha De were their new rulers. The Morrigan was the daughter of Death by Iron. In much later stories she shows up called Morgan le Fey, the wicked witch of Arthurian legend.

5 Macha was a sister of the Morrigan – so she was another gruesome goddess. When heads were gathered up after a battle, people called them "Macha's acorn crop". Heads were displayed on stakes known as "Macha's pillars". But she wasn't all bad, because as we saw in Top Ten story number two, she was happy to help Crunnchu – provided he didn't ask questions or tell anyone about her.

The Morrigan and Macha had another sister. The three of them used to hang around battlefields in the form of crows, scavenging on the flesh of dead bodies.

6 Angus Og, or Young Angus, was the son of Dagda, and he was the Irish god of love. His kisses took the form of four lovely birds, who always fluttered round his head. He fell in love with a girl called Caer, but was told he could not be with her because every other year she turned into a swan. When the year turned, he went and found her and turned himself into a swan so he could be with her. They flew together to his palace on the River Boyne, making the most beautiful swans' song together. Angus was the dad of Dermot, who ran off with Grania (see page 142).

7 Lugh★ Long Arm was a grandson of Diancecht, the physician who went ballistic when Miach healed

★ loo

Nuada. Lugh's name means "the Shining One". Lugh's dad was Cian, one of the sons Diancecht *didn't* kill, and his mum was a Formorian woman called Ethniu.

Lugh arrived at the royal court at Tara when Nuada Silver Arm was holding a feast. The gatekeeper asked what skill he possessed. He replied, "I am a wheelwright."

"We already have one of those," said the guard.

"I am a blacksmith."

"We have one of those too."

"I am a physician."

"And one of those."

"A poet."

"And one of those."

On and on it went, Lugh, the all-skilful, listing his accomplishments, and the guard saying, "Sorry mate, nothing doing."

Finally Lugh said, "But do you have anyone else who can do *all* of these things?"

The gatekeeper must have been a bit thick, because he hadn't thought of that. He now allowed Lugh to enter, and when Nuada saw him he knew at once that this was the man who would lead the Tuatha De Danaan to victory against the Formorians. His spear was one of the Tuatha De's four sacred objects.

8 Manannan Mac Lir was god of the sea. He was a great conjuror and trickster, who sometimes showed up at court with his shoes full of water, and seemed, like the sea, to be able to get in and out wherever he wanted. When he was not travelling, he lived in the Isle of Man (which is named after him) on a mountain shrouded in mist. If anyone ever tried to conquer the island, he brought the mist down all over it. As a result, the island was never conquered, not even by the Romans. Even today it is an independent part of the United Kingdom.

9 Ogma was another son of the Dadga. He was the god of strength and also the god of poetry – that's why he's often called Cermaid Honeymouth, because sweet words fell from his tongue.

Ogma invented Ogam, which was a bit like a secret code, carved on trees. The very first message he carved was a message to Lugh Long Arm on a birch rod, warning him to beware in case beings from the Otherworld stole his wife away.

10 Eire or **Eriu** was the wife of a grandson or maybe a great-great grandson of the Dagda. She was queen when Amergin White-Knee led the Milesians to victory over Danu's tribe. Actually, she was one of three goddess-queens. Amergin did a deal with all of them – that if

they made peace, the country would be called by their names. Eire must have been very special, because he promised her that Eire would be the country's name for ever. So that is why the Irish name for Ireland *is* Eire!

Legend 3: Nera and the Otherworld

Top ten story number three also comes from *The Cattle Raid of Cooley*. The hero of the story, Nera, was a warrior at the court of Queen Maev, a fierce, warlike queen, who stood no nonsense from anyone, not even her husband, Ailill.

It's a really creepy story about what happened one Samhain eve. Samhain was the Celtic New Year, and the night before the gates of the Otherworld opened wide so that dead men walked the earth and the living disappeared if they went too near the old sidhs (seeths) or burial mounds.

So here, specially for Top Ten readers, is an episode of the old Celtic soap opera, Sidhside. In the last episode, Queen Maev hung two troublemakers. Their bodies are hanging from the gibbet – but they just won't die, and something has to be done about them. . .

SIDHSIDE, EPISODE 427

1. Outside the walls of Cruachan Castle. Night.

Creepy Music. Two bodies swing from a gibbet, which creaks under their weight. A nightwatchman shudders as he scurries past.

CUT TO

2. Interior of Cruachan Castle banqueting hall. Night.

This is more like a barn than a banqueting hall. It is lit by candles and the light of a huge fire. At the wooden table sit Maev, Queen of Connacht, and her consort, Ailill, surrounded by their court. They wear fine clothes, and on the table are dishes of silver and gold, all intricately carved with horned figures and animals.

Maev: Welcome one and all. It's Samhain, we all know what that means. Doors to the Otherworld are open wide.

Ailill: The dead can come and go as they please. So watch it. Everything all right at the gate, watchman?

Nightwatchman: The gate's barred, sir. Trouble is, the danger's inside.

Ailill: What d'you mean?

Nightwatchman: Them corpses sir. The ones you hanged. They're moaning, sir.

Ailill: Moaning?

Nightwatchman: Yes, sir.

Maev: They're after you, Ailill.

Nightwatchman: Aye, ma'am. They are.

Ailill: No problem. I know a cure. You take some twigs from the sacred willow tree and tie them round the dead man's ankles.

Fergus: (*nervously*) It'll take a brave man to do that on Samhain Eve.

Nera: The dead play rotten tricks on Samhain night.

Maev: But this court is full of brave men. Isn't it?

An uncomfortable silence from the courtiers.

Ailill: Of course it is. I say so. And anyway, the man who does it can have anything he wants.

Fergus: Anything?

Maev: Yes. The Queen of Connacht isn't mean.

Connor: Then I will go.

Second Man: And I.

Third Man: And I.

Suddenly there is a scrum as men rush for the door.

CAMERA FOLLOWS THEM OUT INTO. . .

3. Exterior Cruachan Castle. Night.

The men rush to a willow tree, and begin cutting off branches.

Nera: Hang on! Don't hurt the tree. One bracelet is enough. We'll take turns.

Connor: Me first.

Fergus: No, me!

Connor: I spoke first.

Nera: Yeh. He did.

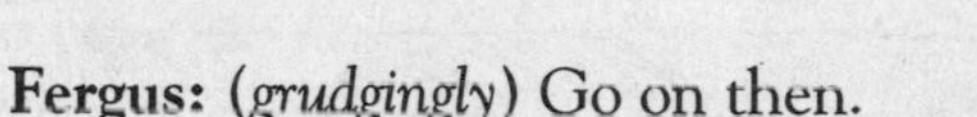

Fergus: (*grudgingly*) Go on then.

Connor takes the bracelet of twigs, and moves cautiously towards the rampart where one of the men is hanging. The others watch fearfully from a distance.

CLOSE-UP SHOT OF CONNOR APPROACHING THE MAN.

As he approaches the body swings, the gibbet creaks, and there seems to come from the corpse a kind of moan. Connor drops the bracelet and runs screaming in terror.

Nera: (*to Fergus*) Your turn.

Fergus: (*teeth chattering*) No, it's OK. After you.

Nera: All right.

He closes his eyes briefly as if offering a prayer to the gods, then walks steadily towards the ramparts. On the way to the gibbet he stoops to pick up the bracelet which Connor dropped. Then he moves towards the dead man.

CLOSE-UP OF THE DEAD MAN'S HEAD.

It seems he raises it, leers and gives a sinister wink. The gibbet creaks. An owl hoots.

CLOSE-UP OF NERA LOOKING PALE AND SCARED.

He reaches out and binds the man's ankles with his woven willows.

Nera: (*muttering to himself*) Almost, almost –

Then, just as he pulls back, his task complete, the bracelet springs apart.

Nera: (*a cry of irritation*) No!

Corpse: Ha ha ha! Trick or treat?

Fergus: (*hand to his face in terror*) He laughed! I heard him laugh!

Connor: Come away, Nera –

But Nera is already tying the bracelet once more.

Nera: No. Not till the job's done. There you are, pal. That should lay your ghost.

Again the bracelet springs open. Now the corpse speaks. Nera jumps back as if he has been bitten by a snake.

Corpse: What you'd be needing is a peg to hold it.

Nera: (*white with fear*) Who spoke? Was that you?

Corpse: What you'd be needing is a peg to hold it.

Nera: A peg. Yes. A peg, um. . .

Corpse: There's one lying there on the ground by your foot.

Nera: (*looking down, shaking like a leaf*) S-s-so there is.

He stoops and picks it up, together with the anklet of willow twigs.

Fergus: Come away, Nera. It's not safe.

Nera: I'm coming. (*As he secures the anklet*) Although I think I'm safe enough with you. You seem a very friendly corpse.

Corpse: Aye, and who wouldn't be friendly to the man who puts his soul to rest.

Nera: I'm glad you see it that way.

Corpse: But I have another favour to ask of you.

Nera: What's that?

Corpse: (*wheedling*) I had a terrible thirst when they hanged me, and that thirst is still with me. Take me down from this gibbet. Carry me on your back to somewhere I can get a drink.

Nera: Well – I suppose. If you really want. (*He turns to call to his mates*) Fergus! Connor! I'm just taking this dead feller for a drink!

CAMERA PANS TO THE RAMPARTS WHERE THE OTHERS WERE STANDING. THERE IS NO ONE THERE.

Nera: They've gone! The beggars!

Corpse: Ach, you can't trust anybody these days.

CUT TO

4. A wild and barren hillside.

Nera is trudging up a hill, bent double beneath the weight of the dead man.

Nera: Blimey, you're a weight. How much further?

Corpse: Ach, no distance, no distance at all.

They come to a house, where a man and woman stand with their five children. The woman is holding out a cup of water as if she is expecting them.

Corpse: Water, woman. Give me a drink, for the love of all the gods.

The woman steps forward and puts the cup to the corpse's lips. He takes a great gulp – and then, instead of swallowing it, he spits it out into the faces of the little family. Immediately they all fall down dead.

Nera: What are you doing! What was that for?

Corpse: Ha ha ha ha ha! Trick or treat!

Nera: That's it. That finishes it. You're going back to the gallows where you belong. And I'm going to claim my reward!

Corpse: Ha ha ha ha ha! That's what you think!

CUT TO

5. Exterior Cruachan Castle. Night.

This is hardly recognizable as the place we saw earlier. It has been burned to the ground. Nothing but blackened, smouldering timbers remain. A long line of warriors moves from the castle to the sidh mound. They are carrying the heads of all the people Nera knew – Maev, Ailill, Fergus, Connor. As Nera approaches this scene he cannot believe his eyes. He lets the dead man slip from his shoulders and watches in horror.

Nera: (*aghast at the sight of a severed head*) Fergus? Is that my old friend Fergus?

Otherworld warrior: Who are you?

Nera: Who are *you*? What's going on?

Otherworld warrior: There's one here escaped!

Second Otherworld warrior: Kill him.

Corpse: No. He's a brave man. Let him live.

Otherworld captain: Take him prisoner. We'll take him to the king.

Nera's hands are tied and he is led towards the mound of the sidh.

Nera: We're going in there? But that's sacred ground. It's the Otherworld.

Otherworld warrior: And we come from the Otherworld, foolish fellow.

He shoves Nera in front of him through a narrow entrance in the rock.

CAMERA FOLLOWS THEM INTO

6. A magical cave.

This is a beautiful, shimmering, glistening place. At the far end of the cave sits the king, on a throne. The warriors are placing the heads of Nera's people in a row on the ground in front of him. They lead Nera to him.

Otherworld warrior: He is also from the Castle of Cruachan, sir.

King: Is that so? How did you escape killing?

Nera: I was carrying the hanged man to get a drink.

King: On Samhain too. You are a brave fellow. (*To the Otherworld Warrior*) Take him to Eithne. She will look after him. (*To Nera*) You are my guest. On one condition.

Nera: What's that?

King: You bring me a bundle of firewood every day.

Nera: Anything you say, sir.

CUT TO

7. Woodland glade.

Nera being jostled along by the Otherworld warrior towards a woodland cottage.

Otherworld warrior: She's a beautiful woman. Just you make sure you keep your hands off her.

As he is speaking, Eithne appears at the cottage door. She is a lovely young woman. She and Nera look into each other's eyes.

Nera: I'll do my best.

MIX TO SAME SCENE A FEW MONTHS LATER.

Now the scene looks idyllic, trees in blossom, sun and shadow on the grass. Nera tying together a bundle of wood which he's chopped. Eithne comes out of the cottage, and offers him a cup of water. He sits down to drink it. She strokes his head. He look up at her lovingly, and she smiles down at him. It is clear they are in love.

Eithne: I love you.

Nera: And I love you.

CUT TO

8. Interior Eithne's cottage.

Nera sits by the fire, looking sad and preoccupied. Eithne, who is spinning wool, looks over at him.

Eithne: You look sad.

Nera: I'm happy with you, my love.

Eithne: But?

Nera: It's when I think of my people – all dead. Eithne, my heart breaks.

Eithne: (*softly*) They are not dead, Nera.

Nera: They are. I saw them with my own eyes.

Eithne: That was a trick of Samhain night. Your people are still seated at the same feast – waiting for you to come back, my love, from tying the willow anklet on the dead man's feet.

Nera: But how can that be? Months have passed since then.

Eithne: No. Not a moment has passed in the mortal world since you cut down the dead man from the scaffold.

Nera: But I don't get it. I saw the palace burnt. My people dead.

Eithne: That was a warning of what will come to pass unless –

Nera: Unless what?

Eithne: Promise you won't tell anyone what I'm going to say?

Nera: Promise.

Eithne: Queen Maev and Ailill must destroy the sidh mound at Cruachan. Go back and tell them. Destroy the Cruachan mound this time next year and nick the crown that's kept there.

Nera: But Eithne – I can't leave you. Not with a baby on the way.

Eithne: When you come back, he'll be a fine boy.

Nera: Anyway, you'll be in trouble when the king finds out I'm gone.

Eithne: He won't know. I'll take your firewood for you every day.

Nera: Why do you risk so much for me?

Eithne: I love you, Nera. Quick. I'll take you to the sidh. That's as far as I can go.

CUT TO

9. Exterior, sidh mound.

It is the same, dark misty night as before. Nera squeezes through the cleft in the rock. For a moment he holds on to Eithne's unseen hand, the other side of the rock. Next the bowl of fruit is passed out to him.

Nera: I will be back next Samhain eve. I swear. I swear.

As he speaks an owl hoots. Now he runs swiftly towards the castle.

CUT TO

10. Interior, Cruachan Castle banqueting hall.

CLOSE-UP OF NERA AS HE PUSHES OPEN THE DOOR.

Disbelievingly, he sees the feast still underway.

NOW CAMERA TAKES HIS POINT-OF-VIEW,

AND SEES WHAT HE SEES.

Everyone is unconcerned. Ailill spots him.

Ailill: So Nera! Did you succeed?

Nera: Yes, my lord.

Maev: Is that fruit? At this time of year? Where did you get it?

Nera: Yes. Oh, I have such a tale to tell. I have visited the Otherworld.

Maev: Is it true?

Ailill: Hey, come and tell us, Nera.

Nera approaches the high table and offers Queen Maev the fruit.

Nera: This is for you, madam. But with it comes a terrible warning.

Ailill: Bring mead for this man. Speak.

A servant brings a metal cup of mead for Nera. Another brings a chair.

THE CAMERA PULLS BACK AND TAKES IN THE WHOLE HALL.

Around Nera, men and women gather, and listen, anxious-faced, to what he has to say.

TITLE MUSIC, ROLL CREDITS.
Over the top of the music the announcer's voice can be heard.

Announcer: And if you want to know what happened to Nera and Eithne and the sidh mound at Cruachan, tune in next week at the same time and watch the next exciting episode of *Sidhside*.

Next Samain, Maev and Ailill destroyed the *sidh* at Cruachan and took the Tuatha De crown for themselves. Nera went back to see Eithne and his child. He could hardly bear to leave them again, but he was scared to stay and give up life as a mortal man. Finally he left – but as he went, a young calf belonging to Eithne sensed everyone's misery, and bellowed so loudly that the great bull called the Findbennach which belonged to Ailill, attacked it. As the calf lay dying, it continued to bellow. Queen Maev asked a Druid priest what it was saying. The Druid answered that the calf was telling them all that if its father, the great Donn of Cooley, had come to his rescue, then the Findbennach would have been beaten. This whetted Queen Maev's appetite. She wanted to own a bull that could beat her husband's. Nothing would satisfy her till she owned the great Donn of Cooley.

So that's how the war between Ulster and Connacht began.

Top Facts 3: Creepy beliefs

1 The Otherworld. If you were a Celt this was as real to you as the everyday world of milking cows and hunting deer. It was a magical land where there was no death or decay – sometimes an underground kingdom, beneath hill, lake or sea; sometimes a land far away; sometimes all around but invisible to human eyes – most of the time! But it wasn't always a friendly place, and you couldn't always leave when you wanted.

2 The **sidhs** were a favourite way into the Otherworld. Sidhs were hills quite close to the castle or fort where ordinary humans lived. Strange things happened on the mounds.

In fact, *sidhs* were probably burial mounds. Before that, they may have been the earliest hill forts; later people moved down to live near rivers, but remembered their ancestors who still lived there.

3 Other gates to the Otherworld were watery places like **lakes and bogs**. This made them pretty scary. You would make offerings to the gods or spirits or ancestors here as you passed by, just in case any of them were thinking of kidnapping you. (That's why all sorts of things, from cauldrons and swords to balls of wool and locks of hair dating from Celtic times, have been found in bogs.)

4 Samhain was the special time of year when the gates to the Otherworld were wide open. This was the Celtic New Year. Then dead warriors returned to earth and beings from the Otherworld roamed about. Bonfires were lit to guide the returning spirits. Sounds familiar? It should. It was celebrated on the night of October 31st, and lives on in our own Hallowe'en.

5 Shape changing. In the Celtic world, you were never safe from your enemies, because they might appear in any form. Anyone who was divine, or even semi-divine, could change shape at the drop of a hat. The idea was that if you were a god or a Druid you could send your soul out in any form you chose. Even worse, your enemy might change you into some other creature. Then you were stuck.

6 Death wasn't the end if you were a Celt. You believed the human spirit lived on. Graves have been found full of armour, weapons, cauldrons, food and jewellery, which any self-respecting Celt would need in the Otherworld.

7 Your **geas** was something you absolutely must or must not do. You might be born with a geas, or sometimes a *geas* would be laid on you by a Druid priest or a being from the Otherworld. And if you broke your geas it meant death – or worse.

8 Thunderstorms were very scary. Every time they happened you would think that the sky was going to fall – and that meant the end of the world to the Celts.

9 You wouldn't like **aspen trees** much either. Why? Because aspen was used to measure graves and corpses – and people could put a bad spell on you by hitting you with a twig or wand of aspen.

10 You would also be scared of the number **13**. Why? Because when a Celtic chief rode into battle, he had three warriors in front of him, three behind, and two either side. If you count all those up, plus the Chief and his charioteer, it comes to twelve. But you knew there was always another riding beside you – and his name was Death!!!

Legend 4: Cuchulain, a top Irish hero!

Cuchulain was one of the most famous of all the Irish heroes. He was a bit like the Incredible Hulk. Whenever he got into a fight, he turned into a mad monster! His hair stood on end, sparks flew from it, weird things happened to his eyes, and he fought like a tiger.

Cuchulain saved Ulster in the terrible years when all the men of Ulster were weak from Macha's curse. Top Ten story number four comes to you as a pull-out magazine supplement – Cuchulain's life in pictures.

To commemorate the victory of Cuchulain and the men of Ulster over the forces of Queen Maev of Connaught, the Irish Messenger presents an 11 page pull-out picture supplement celebrating the life of the great Cuchulain

At last the war between Ulster and Connaught is over. King Conchobar has routed Queen Maev and her hordes. And everyone agrees that Ulster owes her victory to one man – the great hero Cuchulain.

He fought for Ulster, but he was not an Ulsterman by birth. So at the time when all Ulsterman were weak and helpless as women in labour, and it seemed there was no one to stop the wicked Queen Maev from killing our people and stealing our cattle, one man stood between Ulster and disaster.

That man was Cuchulain. Here we pay tribute to the great hero in this special pull-out picture supplement.

Dechtire, sister of King Conchobar, was mother to the great hero.

Dechtire disappeared without trace for seven years, and when she returned to Conchobar's court she had with her a young boy called Setanta. Dechtire said the child was hers – and that his father was none other than Lugh Long-Arm, the god of light!

An early picture of Setanta when he was ready for a fight. All his life, anger changed the great hero into a monster who terrified his enemies.

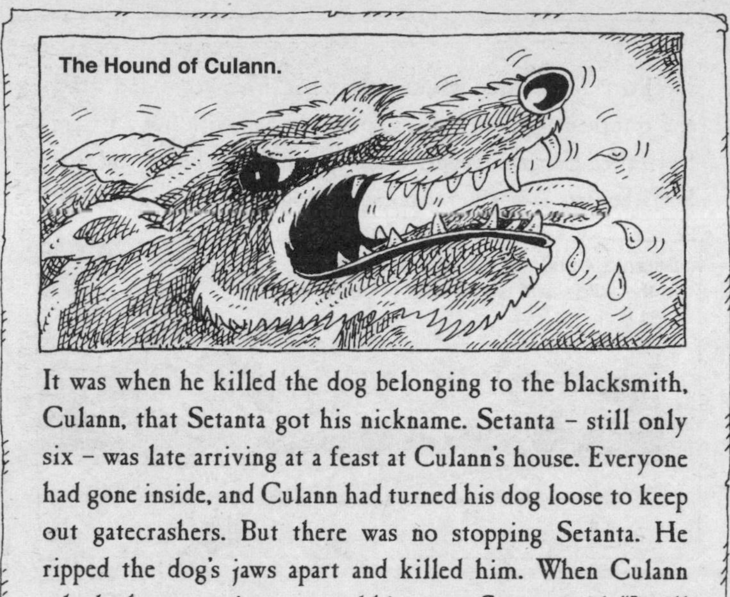

It was when he killed the dog belonging to the blacksmith, Culann, that Setanta got his nickname. Setanta – still only six – was late arriving at a feast at Culann's house. Everyone had gone inside, and Culann had turned his dog loose to keep out gatecrashers. But there was no stopping Setanta. He ripped the dog's jaws apart and killed him. When Culann asked who was going to guard him now, Setanta said, "I will – at least until another pup grows up." Ever afterwards he was known as the Hound of Culann – Cuchulain.

By the time he was sixteen, CC (Cuchulain) was so handsome that all the women of Ulster were in love with him.

Emer and her scary dad.

CC fell madly in love with Emer – and the two spoke to each other in the magic language of the Druids. Unfortunately Emer's Dad wasn't too pleased. Crafty Forgall filled CC's head with stories of the wild warrior woman, Skatha, who knew more about weapons than anyone else alive.

CC's journey to find Skatha.

In order to win Emer's hand, CC set off to find Skatha – a two thousand mile journey to the Land of Shadows.

The burning wheel which Lugh gave his son to help him find his way across a great marsh.

This is the huge chasm, a thousand feet deep, that CC crossed in two strides. Skatha lived on the other side of it with her daughter, Fearsome Utach. Dozens of men had fallen to their deaths trying reach them.

Her daughter Utach the Fearful had fallen for CC and told him how to conquer her mother.

The terrible spear.

The terrible belly spear which Skatha gave to CC in return for sparing her life. It is held between the bare toes, and fired, usually from under water, at the belly of the enemy. The point opens out into thirty jagged barbs once inside the body.

Skatha taught CC all she knew. Then one day an army of Amazons – fierce women warriors who cut off their right breasts so they wouldn't get in the way of their weapons – came looking for a fight. They were led by Aoife, "the Fair Fury", who was Skatha's sworn enemy. Fearing for his life, Skatha drugged CC and tied him up so he wouldn't get hurt – but CC was so strong that the drugs wore off within an hour. He broke his bonds and joined the battle.

Amazons come a cropper.

Three Amazon warriors do moonies at Skatha's sons. CC wasn't standing for that. He cut off the heads of some of the Amazons and presented them to Skatha.

An artist's impression of Cuchulain carrying "the Fair Fury" kicking and screaming to Skatha.

In return for sparing her life, Aoife made peace with Skatha and became Cuchulain's girlfriend.

The gold bracelet which CC left behind for his son when he parted from Aoife. He placed a geas on her – never to tell anyone who the father of her child was.

CC arriving back at Emain Macha.

When told of the terrifying sight, King Conchobar knew that if CC's battle madness wasn't cooled, he would kill everyone in the city. He ordered twelve naked women to stand at the gates of the town. When CC saw them, his blood began to cool. But it took three duckings in cold water before he was completely calm once more.

Wedding day.

CC and Emer on their wedding day. Emer's dad had hoped CC would die abroad, so CC had to kidnap Emer before he could marry her.

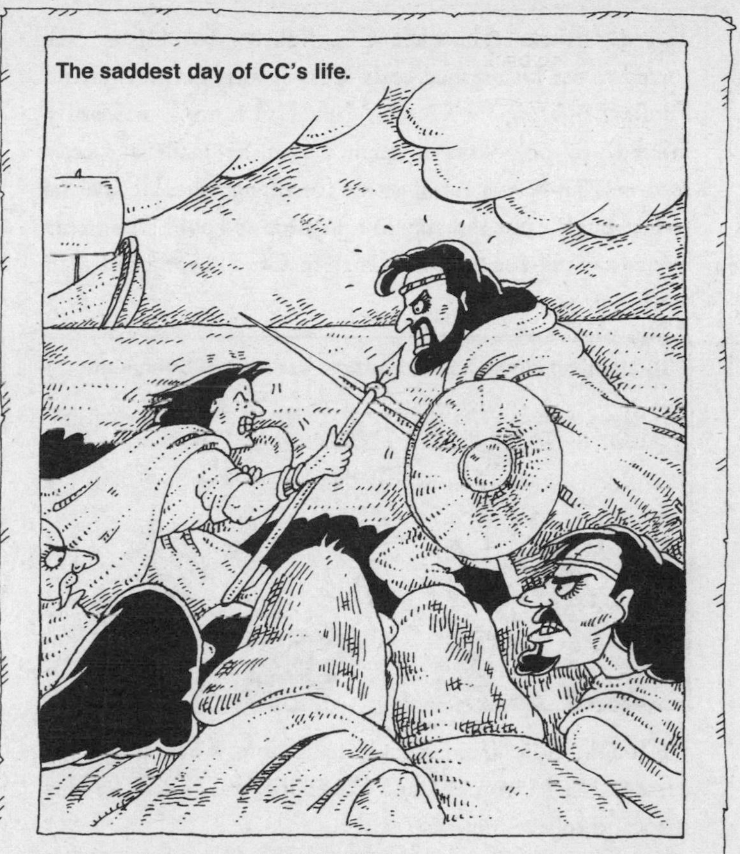

An artist's impression of CC's young son's welcome in Ireland. Aoife, jealous of CC's happiness with Emer, sent the boy to Cuchulain, knowing the reception he would get. Because of the geas the boy did not know who he was. The child defeated two of the king's warriors, and then fought his father. Neither could defeat the other, and finally their battle took them into the sea. There the child held his father's head beneath the waves, until finally a desperate CC fired the dreaded belly spear, killing the child.

Tragedy struck again when CC, fighting for Ulster, was forced to use his dreaded belly spear against his great friend Ferdiad, fighting for Queen Maev. CC himself was badly injured. To onlookers it seemed that he made a speedy recovery, but he was out of action for a long time. He says his father, Lugh, came and sang him to sleep and put herbs on his wounds – and fought for Ulster in CC's shape until such time as he was better.

CC standing single-handed against the men of Connaught.

He fought alone from Samain to Imbolc, when at last the curse of Macha wore off, and Conchobar was able to lead his troops to relieve him.

CC as he is today, with his wife Emer.

Top Facts 4: Give us a job!

Here are three application forms – for the jobs of Priest, Bard and King in Celtic Ireland. See if you can guess which one is which and see if *you* make the grade for any of them.

JOB A

1 Do you have any physical or mental disabilities?

2 Do you always tell the truth?

3 Are you a good leader?

4 Can you use a spear?

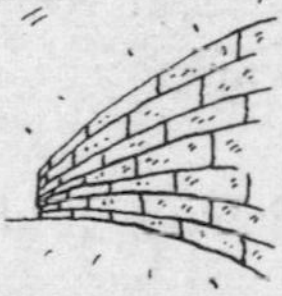

5 Can you vault a three metre wall?

6 Are you loyal to your comrades?

7 Are you brave?

8 Are you a good judge of character?

9 Do you have the gift of second sight? (In other words, can you see into the future?)

10 Can you understand the Ogam code?

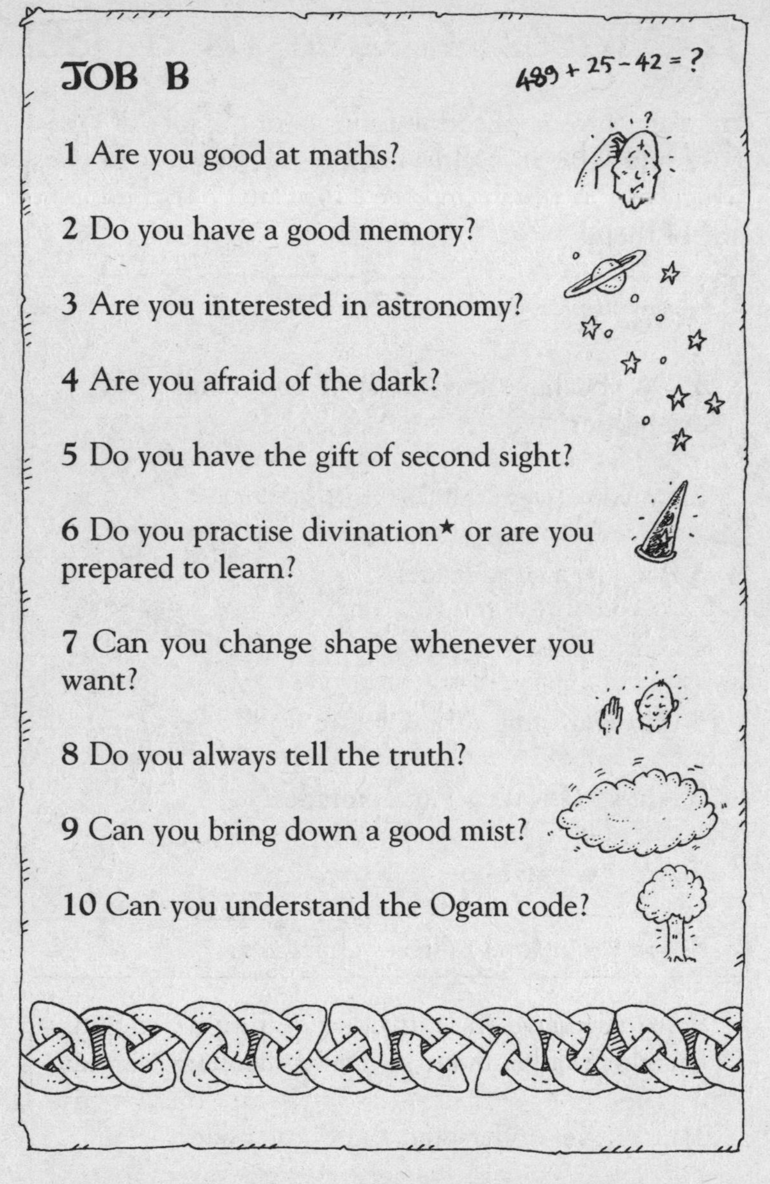

JOB B

1 Are you good at maths?

2 Do you have a good memory?

3 Are you interested in astronomy?

4 Are you afraid of the dark?

5 Do you have the gift of second sight?

6 Do you practise divination★ or are you prepared to learn?

7 Can you change shape whenever you want?

8 Do you always tell the truth?

9 Can you bring down a good mist?

10 Can you understand the Ogam code?

★ Divination is telling the future by reading signs in nature, or going into a trance while wearing horns or a bull's skin.

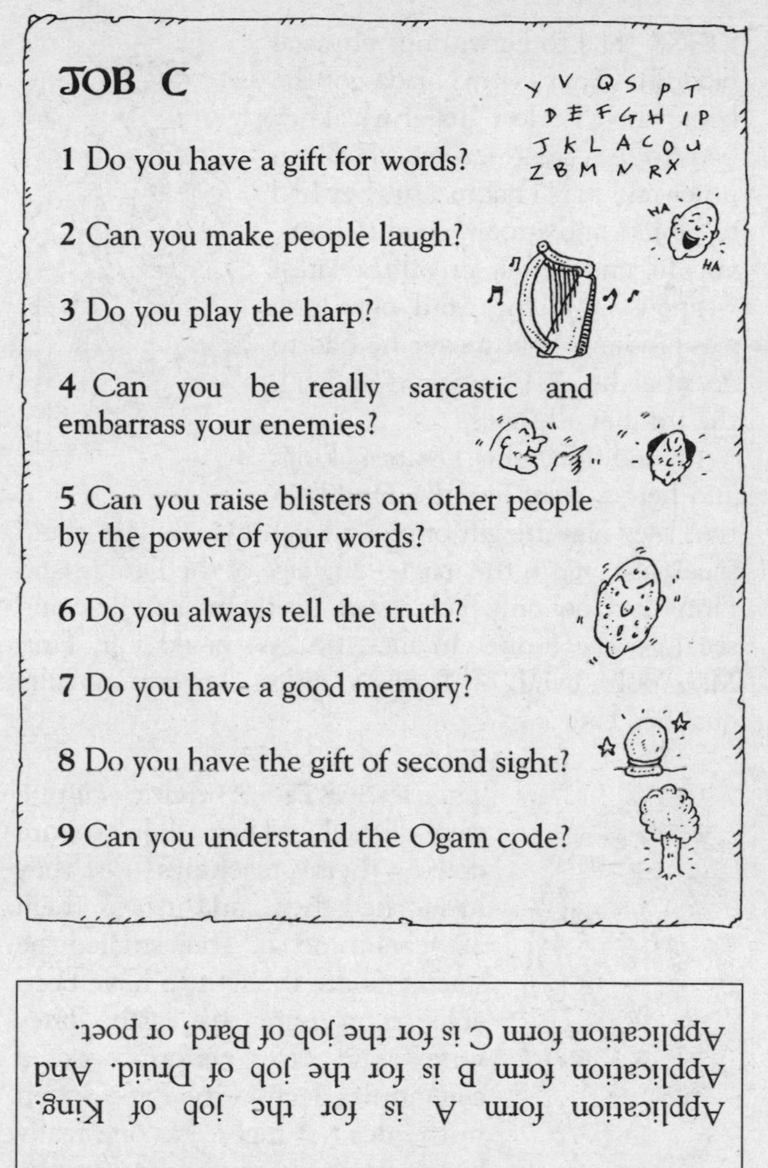

JOB C

1 Do you have a gift for words?

2 Can you make people laugh?

3 Do you play the harp?

4 Can you be really sarcastic and embarrass your enemies?

5 Can you raise blisters on other people by the power of your words?

6 Do you always tell the truth?

7 Do you have a good memory?

8 Do you have the gift of second sight?

9 Can you understand the Ogam code?

Answers – and some explanations

Application form A is for the job of King. Application form B is for the job of Druid. And Application form C is for the job of Bard, or poet.

KINGS had to be without physical blemish. (That's why Nuada got the boot when he lost his arm). They had to be great leaders, both in peace and war. That meant they had to be just and strong, good fighters, very fit, and well up on all the latest weapons. And the word of a king was binding. That meant he had to do what he said he would and tell the truth at all times.

In addition, the greatest kings and heroes were like the Druids in that they had the gift of second sight. Cuchulain could speak to Emer in the magic language of the Druids, and Finn MacCool only had to suck his thumb and he could see into the future. In fact, no one could join Finn MacCool's band of Fenians unless he was a fully qualified bard.

The **PRIESTS** of Celtic culture were Druids. They didn't write down their teachings – they memorized them, and it took them 20 years to do so. They studied the stars, and are thought to have been able to measure the earth. They were said to perform sacred ceremonies deep in the forest, often in the dead of night. No one really knows what the priests did, but tree magic was very important. A

Roman called Pliny the Elder says they cut a sprig of mistletoe growing up an oak tree with a golden sickle – and then used the mistletoe for magic potions.

A good Druid would have all sorts of magical powers, like being able to foretell the future, change shape, and bring down magic mists to confuse their enemies. They spoke a secret language not understood by ordinary folk. Both men and women could be Druid priests. They were holy people, and so it mattered that their word could be trusted, which was why they had to tell the truth.

BARDS were the storytellers, pop-singers, soothsayers and spin doctors of Celtic times all rolled into one. Like the priests, they trained for years, and had to know how to tell all the old stories. In fact, though not priests, they also came from the Druid caste and spoke the same mysterious language.

Bards were considered so important that the ransom price of a captured bard was equal to that of a king. This was because the Celts understood how powerful words are. They knew that storytellers could alter the way people understood what was going on around them, make the enemy look ridiculous and even, in some cases, bring him – or her – out in blisters. And because their words were so powerful, they, like kings and priests, had to stick to the truth rather than made-up stories.

Bards were also the lawyers of old Ireland. As such

they became so powerful, that eventually everyone got fed up with them. They used language so difficult that no one but another bard could understand. The king lost patience and ordered that from then on all stories should be told in the language that ordinary people spoke.

So if YOU want to apply for any of these jobs, you will have to tell the whole truth and nothing but the truth all the time.

WHAT IS THE OGAM CODE?

Ogam was a secret way of writing. It was a series of straight lines, carved on wood. Variations in what wood was used and in the number of lines meant different things.

The wood of the aspen tree was unlucky. So if you wanted to put a bad spell on someone, you carved a curse in Ogam on a piece of aspen and hit him with it.

If you were under a spell, you could be released if your name was carved in Ogam on a piece of wood from an elder tree.

Ogam was also used for detective work. When Etain was carried away by Midir (see Top Ten legend number five) the King's Druid worked out where she was by using four wands of yew and the Ogam code.

Sometimes the Ogam worked like a compass. The son of the King of Alba★ bought his life from Cuchulain by giving him a rod carved with Ogam. The rod led Cuchulain's boat exactly where he wanted it to go.

Ogam was carved on gravestones. If it was rude

★ The old name for Scotland

Ogam, the stone or wooden pole was buried underground, so no one could read it.

Legend 5: Etain and Midir

One of the most romantic stories of Irish legend is that of Etain and Midir. In it, Etain, a beautiful young girl, is wooed by a being from the Otherworld. He knows – though she does not – that in another lifetime she was his wife. He has never stopped loving her, and he wants to claim her. Here coming in as Top Ten number five is Etain's diary, starting with the day a mysterious stranger appears in her life.

My Secret Diary

By Etain, daughter of Etar, age 15

(PRIVATE – DO NOT READ)

35 days after Beltain

Went swimming in the river

-with my friends. The weirdest thing happened. A guy came by on a white horse. He was amazing looking. He had long gold hair held back by a gold band, and he was wearing a green tunic embroidered in red.

All the other girls started nudging each other and giggling and acting really stupid. Deirdre came out of the water with her shift clinging to her, showing everything she'd got — but this guy just stared at ME!

Then he started speaking and everyone went quiet.

ME

I couldn't really understand most of what he said. He said I was alive today as Etain, daughter of Etar, but that once I had "healed the king's eye from a sacred well". Then he said something about how I was swallowed from a cup by my mother. I didn't know what he was talking about. He said, "You don't remember me do you?", and he looked really sad. Then he rode off. All the girls started teasing me, "Ooooh, Etain, what have you been up to?", that sort of thing. And I felt really strange. 'Cos there was something familiar about him, as if I'd seen him before. More than that, actually. As if I'd known him very well. But I can't remember where or when.

Beltain plus 36 (aka 7th June)

Weird dreams last night. First I saw this huge dragonfly, it was so beautiful, wings like gossamer. And it landed on the guy I saw yesterday. He was so gentle with it, he stroked it and held it in his hand. And I could tell the dragonfly really liked being held by him.

Next thing I heard this woman screaming with anger. I couldn't see her, but I was scared. She was in a real rage. And then somehow I was the dragonfly, and I was being buffeted in terrible gales. The sky was full of grey storm clouds, it was cold and raining, and I kept being dashed against rocks and gorse. Then it was as if the wind was pulling me down into the sea. And I ended up on a rock, and my wings were wet and I was cold. Then I woke up.

Beltain plus 37 (aka 8th June)

Keep thinking about the guy in the green tunic. Who is he? Where do I know him from? More important, how can I get to know him better? I've asked some of the local lads if they know who he is, but they're so mean and bigheaded, they just keep teasing me. Talking about Etain's "hot date", that sort of thing. I hate them. Wish I didn't blush so easily.

Beltain plus 40 (aka 11th June)

Guess what? So much for all

the lousy males round here. The High King of Ireland is looking for a wife, so he sent some men round looking for the most beautiful girl in the land. And out of all the girls in Ireland, they chose me! Now my mother says Eochy is coming to see for himself.

Think I'd better wash my hair. What if he turns out to be the guy in the green cloak!??!! Oh, how I hope he does!

Beltain plus 41 (aka 12th June)

I can't believe it. I'm getting married — to the High King! I'm so excited, I don't know where to start.

Yesteday I went down to the stream at Bri Leith to wash my hair. I'd just started taking all the little gold beads from the ends of my hair, and combing it with the silver comb Dad gave me last Lughnasa. And lo and behold, suddenly I looked up and there this guy I realized must be the High King. He wasn't the guy in the green cloak, he was much older, but he looked OK.

So next thing I knew he'd asked me to marry him. There's a feast to celebrate tonight.

I think I'm pleased. Though it does seem a bit sudden.

Beltain plus 50 days (aka 21st June)

Here I am at Tara, the palace of the High King. It is very posh. Lots of rooms with rushes on all the floors.

I suppose I'm pretty lucky really. Eochy is a nice man. Trouble is, I keep thinking about the other guy. Green Cloak. I told Airmid (my maidservant) and she told me not to be stupid. She told me you can't compare someone you've only seen for a moment on a sunny afternoon with someone you live with all the time. I suppose she's right.

Lughnasa (aka 1st August)

Something weird happened today. A young chieftain I'd never seen before showed up at Tara and asked if he could speak to me alone. So I sent Airmid away. Then he said that my name was Etain, which I obviously knew, but I wasn't really the daughter of Etar, I was some other Etain, AND THAT I HAD BEEN MARRIED TO HIM IN ANOTHER LIFETIME.

"Oh yeh. Sure," I said. I thought he was having me on. But he insisted he wasn't. He said that we <u>had</u> been married, and blissfully happy. So I asked him, if we were so blissfully happy, how come we weren't still together?

Then he told me this great long story. He said he had another wife, called Fuamnach who he had been married to before he was married to me. And apparently Fuamnach was dead jealous of me, because he loved me more than he loved her. So she used her magical power to turn me into a pool of water.

Okay, I asked him, so if I was turned into a pool of water, how did I get to be Etain, daughter of Etar?

Then he told me something that made my hair stand on end. He said that the pool of water changed into a DRAGONFLY !!! He said I'd done it to stay close to him and that he'd cupped me in his hands and stroked me. But Fuamnach knew who I was and screamed and created a storm that blew me away!!! Just like my dream the other night !!! I mean, is that weird or what?

I could have told HIM what happened next. I was blown down on to a deserted shore. Sure enough, that's what he said. But then, according to him, Angus the god of love found me (the poor bedraggled dragonfly) on the pebbly beach. He took me to his place and kept me in a cage. But Fuamnach still hated me so she stole the cage, and threw me out into another storm. Then finally I fell through the smoke hole of Etar's house — — straight into a drink my mother was holding. She didn't notice and swallowed me! All the hairs on my neck were standing up and prickling by this time. Because the guy in the green cloak had said the same thing!!!

Anyway, nine months later I was born as Etain, daughter of Etar.

I must say I was pretty shaken by all this. The only thing I didn't get was why this guy who claimed to be my former husband looked so young. I mean, we must have been married to each other twenty years ago.

"I am Midir, Lord of the Sidh mound of Bri Leith," he said, when I asked him. And he explained that beings from the Otherworld never grow old or die. And then he asked me to come back to the Otherworld with him. He said it was where I belonged.

I got quite scared then. I didn't want to go. I told him I couldn't just up and leave poor Eochy.

He asked me if I loved Eochy.

And then I found myself saying something really strange. It was as if someone else was speaking. I said, "Not as I love you."

"So come away with me," he said.

I was more scared than ever. I didn't want to go with him there and then. I mean, what if he wasn't Midir? I don't want to screw up everything with Eochy if it's all a fairy story. In the end I told him I could only come with him if Eochy gave me his blessing. Which I know he'll never do.

"I'll hold you to that," said Midir. Then he was gone. But since then I haven't been able to stop thinking of him. Because although he didn't look like the guy in the green cloak, I'm almost sure it was him. And it could be. Beings from the Otherworld change shape all the time.

I don't know what's going to happen next. I don't know if I want him to come back or not.

Samhaim minus 11 (aka 21st October)

Midir came back today. This time he didn't just have a look of the guy in the green cloak. He actually WAS him except today he was dressed in a purple tunic. He didn't speak to me, though I caught him gazing at me with those strange grey eyes of his, and my heart started to thump so loudly I thought everyone would hear. My hands were trembling too.

He said he'd come to challenge Eochy to a game of chess. Eochy's mad about chess. He wins every game he plays. He asked Midir what he wanted to play for.

Midir pretended to think. I thought he might come out with what he really wanted – me – but he didn't. Instead he just said the loser should pay whatever the winner asked. Eochy told him he should be careful, he might lose more than he bargained for.

So then they started. Midir was very clever. He let Eochy win. Eochy asked him for fifty grey horses and fifty gold bridles to go with them. Midir didn't bat an eye-lid. He just went off saying he'd be back.

"That's the last we'll see of him," said Eochy.

But I'm not so sure.

Samhaim

Eochy was wrong. Midir came back three days ago with fifty dark-grey horses, all wearing bridles chased with gold, and challenged Eochy to another game.

Eochy won the second game too.

This time he asked Midir for fifty boars, fifty white cows and fifty white calves, fifty grey sheep, and fifty ivory-hilted swords and fifty shining cloaks. I think he thought he was on to a good thing.

Midir disappeared again, but this morning he was back, driving all the animals before him. He caught my eye as he came into the great hall.

"Another game?" he asked Eochy. Eochy was thrilled, he thought he was going to win again. But of course, he lost the third game. I think he was quite scared that Midir was going to ask him for the sort of stuff he'd asked from Midir. But all Midir asked was if he could take me in his arms and kiss me.

Eochy didn't like it. I could tell by the expression on his face. But after the way he'd behaved, he didn't have a lot of choice. In the end he said it was fine for Midir to kiss me, but not today. He told Midir he could have his kiss in a month's time.

When Midir had gone, Eochy asked me if I knew anything about him. Did I want him to kiss me?

Well, by this time the fact is, I did, very much. But I couldn't exactly say that. So I said I only wanted it if Eochy was happy about it.

He told me there was no way Midir was going to get his kiss. He said that when he came back, Tara would be guarded by every warrior in Ireland. And that Midir wouldn't get within a mile of me.

A month later.

All month chieftains and warriors have been arriving, summoned to guard Tara. Eochy hasn't let me out of his sight for days, and today, the day Midir was due to arrive, the gates were barred, and great tree-trunks shoved up against them in case Midir should bring a battering ram.

This morning, I stood with Eochy in the innermost room of the palace, with ring after ring of warriors surrounding us, spears at the ready. I didn't see how anyone could possibly get through to us. I was quite relieved in a way. I do love Midir, but I'm scared of throwing away everything I have here as queen.

Then all of a sudden, as if by magic, Midir was in the centre of all the rings of warriors, along with

Eochy and me. He just appeared out of thin air! I've never seen him look more handsome, not even that first day when he appeared by the river. "I have come to claim my kiss," he told Eochy. Eochy was furious. The warriors had failed to keep Midir out and now he had no choice. He's a king, he had to keep his word.

Suddenly to kiss Midir was the thing I wanted more than anything in the world. I forgot Eochy and all the watching warriors, with their spears and their angry eyes. Midir took me in his arms, and as he kissed me, I was somewhere else - - in his sidh of Bri Leith - a time long ago, or maybe it was never in time at all. I was happy with the man I loved more than any other.

Then I felt Midir lift me in his arms. To my astonishment, I felt us rising through the air, rising, rising, up through the smoke hole high above the fire. In seconds we were above the palace, and below us I could see Eochy and all the servants and warriors running outside and looking up at us.

"Swans!" someone shouted. "They've turned into swans."

I looked at Midir. Sure enough, alongside me, big white wings beating was a huge swan. Then I realized that my arms were covered with white feathers too. They had turned into wings, and my legs into big webbed feet which were folded up beneath my belly.

"They're chained together!" Another voice floated up from the tiny people with their upturned faces far below.

At first I did not know what they meant. Then I saw a fine gold chain around Midir's neck, and realized that the same chain stretched between us and wound around my own neck. And I knew the chain had always been there, you just couldn't see it before. We are bound by love to each other. We'll be married till the end of time.

Top Facts 5: The Otherworld – the ultimate holiday destination

Fancy a holiday where it's summer all the time? Where fresh fruits grow all year round, and the pig that's killed for the cooking pot one night comes to life again next day? Where it never rains unless you ask it to, and then only for as long as you want? An island in the sun where illness, old age, decay and death just don't exist? If this is your idea of paradise, then book now for the holiday of a lifetime in the Otherworld!

This is what tour operators *usually* say in their ads. Yet WHAT HOLIDAY? has been receiving disquieting reports which suggest that the Otherworld is not always what it's cracked up to be. We're not saying don't go – because one day there'll be nowhere else you *can* go. What we are saying is be aware of what you're letting yourself in for...

Here are the ten questions and worries most commonly raised by our readers.

> 1 I would love to go take a holiday in the Otherworld, but where exactly is it? When I ask my travel agent he becomes very vague and comes out with a lot of stuff I dont understand.

I'm not surprised your travel agent comes over vague when you try to pin him down. The fact is, "the Otherworld" means different things to different people. Sometimes it's an underground kingdom, with kings and maidens and bulls all living beneath the old sidhs (pronounced seeths). Sometimes it's underwater, beneath a lake or the sea and it only appears above the waves once in seven years. Other people would say it's nowhere but in our heads – an imaginary place, which exists all the time and which you can always visit.

> 2 I have booked a holiday in the Otherworld starting next month, but my travel agent has still not confirmed the travel arrangements. What should I do?

The reason your travel agent hasn't confirmed the travel arrangements is quite simple. He has no idea how you are going to get there. All he can do is tell you how other people have made the journey.

One way is by slipping through a cleft in a rock up on the sidh. This happens most commonly at Samhain, and this is not necessarily the safest time of year to go. Or you may enter what looks like a perfectly ordinary house and find yourself at an Otherworldly feast, usually with Giobniu, the blacksmith god as your host. At other times, people from the Otherworld simply appear and summon mortals like you and me to join them in the Otherworld. This may involve disappearing into a magic mist, or travelling on a horse who can walk on water or fly through the air. And your travel agent has no say at all in when or how or even whether this will happen for you. The important thing is not to give him any money till you get there.

3 I have always wanted to visit the Otherworld, but I get confused when I hear it called by a lot of different names. Are these all different places? And are they all part of the Otherworld? If so how do we know?

You're right that the Otherworld is called by many different names. The Land Under the Waves, the Land of Youth, Land of the Blessed, the Field of Happiness, the Plain of Two Mists and the Land of

Donn are all names given to the Otherworld.

The reason we know these are all really the same place is because what happens there is the same in all of them. Time as we know it doesn't exist. It's a land of plenty. Great weather, fresh fruits, flowers all year round. Great music. Lots of love, no guilt, no death. In fact, when battles do occur, the warriors are healed of their wounds and/or raised from the dead next day in order to fight again.

4 Whenever I hear the Otherworld being described as a paradise on earth I see red. My son was killed by raiders of the Otherworld two years ago last Samhain. They chopped off his head and took it to their king beneath the sidh. Please warn your readers not to be taken in by all this soft-focus advertising. The otherworld is a cruel place and we mortals should steer clear of it. Do you agree?

I am very sorry to hear about your son. Yes, the Otherworld does have another side to it, although I have to say that for raiders to come and attack the mortal world unprovoked is unusual, though not unheard of. They usually reserve their dark side for attackers or uninvited guests. For instance, if you try to gatecrash the Otherworld – and particularly if you're planning to nick a cauldron or something – it can be a scary place. Then it's called the Land of Shade, and you'll find heads on spikes around the walls, and serpents and monsters, and you'll be lucky to get out alive. In fact, most heroes didn't, and one of the names of the Otherworld is the Land of the Dead, kingdom of Donn.

5 *Please can you tell me if it's true that Samhain is a good time to travel to the Otherworld?*

Quite simply, Samhain is the time of year when beings, mortal (that's us) and immortal (that's them – they never die) can move freely between the two worlds. However, just because it's easy doesn't necessarily mean it's best. The Otherworld is pretty creepy at Samhain. You can't always get out again when you want to. And the ghosts from the Otherworld who are wandering about our world can get up to some strange tricks. They may offer to take you to the Otherworld and lead you up some dark hillside and leave you up to your waist in some cold peat bog. If you really want to go to the Otherworld, it might be better to choose a less dangerous time of year.

6 I've heard it said that the Otherworld is where the Tuatha De Danaan disappeared to when they were defeated by the sons of Mil. Are we just talking about life and death here? Are the sidh mounds just graveyards inhabited by ghosts?

This is an interesting question. It's certainly true that many of the Tuatha De were killed around the hill forts and would have been buried underground. It's also true that others would have escaped by sea, and most of those would have drowned. However, there is nothing pale and ghost-like about the inhabitants of the Otherworld. They are vigorous people who enjoy eating and drinking, music and dancing, and generally having a good time. So the kingdoms beneath the sidh mounds are more than just graveyards – they may be the kingdom of the world beyond death.

7 I would like to relocate to the Otherworld because I like the idea of never dying. However, one thing worries me. If no one dies in the Otherworld, doesn't that mean it will eventually get overcrowded?

No, apparently not. This is because the Otherworld spills over into our world. Otherworld beings are often born as animals and people back in to the earthly world. Besides, I think we can assume that space is more fluid in the Otherworld than it is in our own.

8 MY DAD SAYS THAT THE OTHERWORLD EXISTS OUTSIDE SPACE AND TIME. IS THIS TRUE, AND IF SO, DOESN'T THAT MEAN IT'S JUST AN IMAGINARY PLACE ?

Some people say that the Otherworld exists outside human time. When Nera came back, he thought weeks had passed but he found his people still at supper just as he had left them. Other people think a few years have gone by, but when they return they discover that centuries have passed. As to whether it exists outside space as we know it – there is a lot of argument about this. Some people are very definite that it is a place you go to. Others think it is just another aspect of the everyday world and that a moment's insight can take us there. It's worth thinking about this before you stump up for a package holiday.

9 *Some tour operators claim that Brazil in South America is the original Otherworld. Is this true? If so, how could the Celts have known about it?*

First your question, is it true? Yes and no. The Celts always believed there was a glorious country far away over the sea to the west. They called it Hy Brasil, the Land of the Blessed, and thought of it as part of the Otherworld. When Spanish sailors landed on the continent now known as South America they thought they had found this place, and so it got the name Brazil.

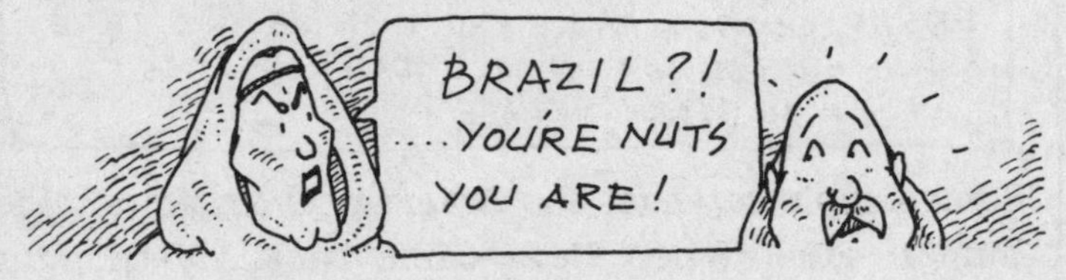

As to how the Celts could have known about it, well, a few years ago a man made a boat out of ox-hide like the coracles which Celts are believed to have used around the coast and rivers of Ireland. He sailed it all the way across the Atlantic. So it is just possible the early Celts did the same thing. Other early peoples also thought – or perhaps knew – that there was land far to the West. The ancient Egyptians called it Venus, the morning star, la Merica, and believed it hung over a great and magic land.

However the land far to the west may have more to do with the fact that all the people who invaded Ireland all came west to do so – the idea of travelling west was familiar to the people.

Whatever you do, don't sign up for one of the ox-hide coracle ferries run by some travel agents. You're extremely unlikely to reach Brazil – though you might find the Otherworld beneath the ocean.

10 *I am very concerned by the use of the word "holiday" in the context of the Otherworld. My older daughter went on one of these so-called holidays to the Otherworld, and never came back. Now my younger daughter says she wants to go, because she likes the idea of staying young and living forever. What should I do?*

This is most people's first reaction. However, your daughter should bear in mind that for ever means for ever. Ask her, will she get bored and miss her old friends and the cycles of the seasons? Also point out to her that her sister has not returned. Is she sure this is because her sister wants to stay there, or is she just not able to get back?

You are absolutely right that the use of the word "holiday" is misleading. Holidays are rests from everyday life, and everyday life resumes when they are over. There is no coming back from this holiday. Going to the Otherworld is a one-way trip. However, the ads are right in one thing: the Otherworld really is "the ultimate destination".

Legend 6: Finn MacCool

Finn MacCool★ was another of the *great* heroes of Irish legend. He was a kind of outlaw, because he didn't come from one of the royal tribes or clans as the hero Cuchulain had. He was known as *ecland*, or clanless. Men like Finn formed outlaw bands known as *Fian* or Fenians, also known as warlords. Finn's father had been killed in battle, and his mother, afraid their enemies would come and kill their baby son, sent him away at birth to be brought up by two Druidesses. Finn actually survived and lived to be 230, and there are many many legends about his long life.

In at number six in our Top Ten Irish Legends is the tale of Finn and a strange visitor from the Otherworld...

★ sometimes MacCumhall

The Ballad of the Little Fawn

The sun was sinking in the west.
Finn and his men headed home to rest,
When out the thicket sprang a doe.
The chase was on! Finn cried, "Let's go!"

Through darkening woods they ran and ran;
Deer, hounds, and following, horse and man.
But horse and man were tired and soon
They lost the deer in the dusky gloom.

Only Finn's hounds could stand the pace.
Bran and Skolawn, with tireless grace,
Loped and leaped behind the fawn;
It seemed they could have run till dawn.

But then, she stopped, the little fawn,
Waited quiet for Bran and Skolawn
Who did not leap and sink their teeth
But licked and nuzzled and rolled beneath.

That night, in Finn's great hall, she lay
Before the fire on reed and hay,
The dogs beside her, cheek by jowl.
If anyone came near, they growled.

Much later, Finn, all alone in bed,
Woke, with dogs pawing at his head,
To see a woman, young and fair,
Who said, "Sir, rescue me from my despair."

"Your name?" said Finn. "Why are you here?"
"I'm Saba," she said. "I am the deer
You chased at dusk. I'm cursed for life
Because I will not become the Dark Druid's wife."

"But you're a girl," said Finn. "You're not a deer."
"Yes, true," she said. "Because I'm here.
In your house, Finn, the Druid has no power.
Please keep me safe with you within this tower."

"Sure you can stay," said Finn. Soon they were wed,
And soon Finn's men were grumbling, cos they said
Finn wouldn't fight or hunt or leave his wife.
He stayed at home to guard her with his life.

But then one day the King of Lochlann's fourteen men
Landed on Ireland's coast to plunder. Then
Finn had to leave his wife and come and fight,
And the dark Druid seized his chance one night.

He came in Finn's shape, had Finn's hounds and horse;
Though Finn was far away fighting the Norse.
Sweet Saba ran to greet him as he waved.
The servants understood too late to save.

Finn's wife was turned back to a fawn.
She followed the Dark Druid that sad morn.
Poor Saba, she was never seen again,
At least not in the world of mortal men.

Yet Saba carried Finn's child in her womb,
And begged the infant should not share her doom.
"Then you must treat him as a human mum,"
The Druid said. "No licking with your tongue."

"I won't," said Saba. But when time came for birth,
For her it was the hardest thing on earth.
She'd been a deer too long. She ached to lick.
Her tongue reached out and gave one sloppy slick.

And in that place there grew a tuft of hair
Just like a deer's. "Lick more!" the Druid dared.
"No," Saba moaned. So he remained a human child,
But naked, cold, unlicked. His mother lay and cried.

And years went by, and still Finn missed his wife.
He searched the hills and woods by day and night.
Beside him loped his hounds, Bran and Skolawn.
He hoped one day they'd find the missing fawn.

They never did. But one day came upon a boy
Naked and cold. They greeted him with joy.
"Who are you, lad? Where are you from?" said Finn.
The boy stared wordless, shrugged and scratched a shin.

They took him home. He had no human speech.
He walked on all fours. He seemed out of reach.
Most strange of all, he had a tuft of hair
Just like a deer's, except that it was fair.

Finn called him "Wild One," and "My little deer".
And over time he learned to speak. Words became clear.
He loved words, played with them, told tales
As he rode beside the great Finn over hills and dales.

One day he had enough words to explain
How he had lived before the day Finn came.
A Dark Man lurked within the glen, he said.
But a kind deer fed him and kept him warm in bed.

Finn took him on his lap and told the tale
Of Saba, his mum, and the Dark Druid's spell.
"That deer was your mother and I'm your dad.
And I'll keep you safe from that harsh, cruel cad."

Finn named him Oisin, his little fawn,
And kept him safe from dusk to dawn,
And dawn to dusk. He taught him fight
And loved his strange son, his life's light.

And the tale's not over, the song's not done,
For Oisin was more than a warrior's son,
Or even a warrior in his own right
Though no man alive could put him to flight.

No, the tale's not over, the song's not done,
For Oisin was more than a warrior's son.
For that wordless fawn-boy grew up to be
The greatest poet in all history.
With a head full of words
And a heart full of tales
He sang Ireland's stories
To sky, hill and vale.

Top Facts 6: Magic birds and animals

As you've probably noticed, shape-changing is common in Irish stories. That's why people could become animals, and vice versa – even if they couldn't always choose when.

They also lived very close to their animals in daily life; they depended on them for wealth, and food, either through breeding or hunting. So they knew far more about animal behaviour and the characteristics of different species than most of us do today. Here are the Celts' top ten animals.

1 The **boar** was admired for the way it would turn and face its attackers when it was being hunted. It was seen as one of the bravest animals. Its meat was also considered the most delicious, and the best cuts were reserved for the top heroes. Top boars: the magic ones, who having gone into the pot one day, were alive the next to be killed again.

2 The **stag** was loved because it would shed its antlers every year and grow new ones the following spring – and because these antlers became bigger and more magnificent with age. Carvings have been found all over the Celtic world showing men sitting cross-legged, wearing a head-dress of antlers and holding a snake. These are probably pictures of magic ceremonies.

3 Bulls were a symbol of fertility and fighting strength. Bulls were sometimes offered in sacrifice to the gods – but not usually until they were old! Druid priests wrapped themselves in bull skins in order to get in touch with the spirits.

4 Horses were really popular with Irish kings who were mad about horse-racing. Unlike other animals, horses were never killed for food, and were carefully buried when they died. Macha has been called the horse goddess – maybe that's why she could outrun King Conchobar's horses.

5 Swans were signs of good luck, and a swan with a golden chain around its neck symbolized a faithful lover, transformed by a jealous rival. The most famous were the children of King Lir, turned into swans by their jealous stepmother, and cursed to remain like that for thousands of years. They sang so beautifully that people came from far and wide to listen to them.

6 Ravens and **crows** were birds of bad omen; the Morrigan, the battle goddess of the Celts, visited battlefields disguised as a raven and scavenged on dead flesh. To this day, some people think ravens are a sign of death.

7 Cranes were also considered unlucky if you met them as you went into battle. The most famous crane was a young girl called Aoife, transformed by her rival in love, Iuchra. Aoife was cursed to remain a crane for three hundred years; then, when she died, Manannan Mac Lir, god of the sea, took her skin and made it into a bag. In this bag he kept all his great treasures – the King of Scotland's shears, and the King of Lochlann's helmet, a belt made from the skin of the great whale and the bones of Asail's swine. And whoever had that bag was the greatest and most powerful hero in Ireland.

8 Cats were sinister. They were never kept as pets – perhaps because the cats of Celtic Europe were like the fierce, wild cats of Scotland today.

Cats kept their bad reputation down the centuries. Right up to the eighteenth century they were associated with witches.

9 Dogs are always called **hounds** in Irish legend. They were hunting dogs – and when they weren't out hunting with their masters, they were allowed to wander loose about the fort or castle, ready to attack intruders. The hound of Culann, who was killed by Cuchulain, was one such killer dog.

10 Hares were considered lucky – the Irish believed that they brought Spring up out of the ground by their leaping. The Druids worked out what would happen in the future by the direction in which hares ran.

Legend 7: The bewitching of Finn MacCool

After Finn MacCool killed the King of Lochlann in battle, he brought up the king's son, Midac, as his own. Midac never forgave Finn for killing his dad and used his time in Finn's house to spy on him. Finn got wise to this, and offered Midac – now 16 – good land to leave his house. Midac went, and for the next 14 years, Finn never clapped eyes on him – though people said agents from Lochlann passed through Midac's kingdom on their way to spy on Finn. Then one day, Finn was out hunting, when a dark stranger invited him to come to supper.

This is the cast of Top Ten story number seven – our comic strip *Slaughter at the Ford.*

Slaughter At The Ford

One day, Finn and his men were out hunting when a dark stranger invited him to supper.....

HE MEANS NO GOOD.

BUT FREE NOSH!

LET'S GO AND CHECK OUT HIS PAD.

NOT ALL OF US. SOME OF US SHOULD STAY BEHIND. FIACHNA, INNSA, DERMOT.

So Dermot and co. hid in the woods while Finn and his men went to the castle.

LOOK AT THIS!

BUT THERE'S NO ONE HERE!

LET'S TUCK IN.

As they tucked in, they realised the dark stranger was watching them coldly.

MINE HOST?

DOESN'T SAY MUCH IF HE IS.

Then he turned and left the hall. The fire and the warmth, the light and the food went with him.

IT'S DARK.

IT'S COLD.

WHAT HAPPENED - I WAS EATING THAT.

I CAN'T MOVE. I'M STUCK.

He wasn't the only one. All the men of the Fianna were stuck hard to the cold earth floor.

SUCK YOUR THUMB, FINN-WHAT DO YOU SEE?
So Finn sucked his magic thumb.
BAD NEWS LADS, THE STRANGER'S MIDAC. AND HE'S BRINGING THE MEN OF LOCHLANN TO KILL US ALL.
PITY YOU DIDN'T THINK OF SUCKING YOUR THUMB BEFORE.
WHAT ARE WE GOING TO DO?
WE'RE GOING TO SING, LAD. THE BATTLE SONG OF THE FIANNA

★ A song sung for the dead.

...But finally ...Innsa lost his head.
TAKE THAT!
AAARRRGHH GROANNNN
WHAT'S HAPPENING?
WHO GOES THERE?
FRIEND OF YOURS!
YOU KILLED MY FRIEND! YOU'RE FOR IT, MATE
DON'T YOU WORRY, INNSA, NO ONE'S NICKING YOUR HEAD I'LL PUT IT BACK WITH YOUR BODY.

Fiachna buried Innsa standing up, looking towards the enemy, with his head stuck on his neck. No sooner had he finished, when Midac's men appeared.
BIFF!
BOUNCE!
THWACK!
Soon the river was blocked with bodies.
AAARGH!
AAARGH!
I'VE GOT YOU MIDAC'S HEAD HERE, FINN.

GOOD MAN, DERMOT — BUT IT'S NOT ENOUGH.
NOT ENOUGH?!!
NO. TO BREAK THIS SPELL I NEED THE BLOOD OF THE THREE KINGS FIGHTING WITH MIDAC.
NO PROBLEM I'LL GET THEM FOR YOU.
Will Dermot succeed in killing the three kings or will they kill him? Will their blood release Finn from Midac's terrible spell? OR — horror of horrors — is he stuck there forever?

Top Facts 7: Ireland, AD100

Your school has arranged an exchange visit through time to visit Ireland, AD100. Here we tell you what you can expect on your trip through time – and the ways you can make your visit more enjoyable.

1 First of all, you can expect a good welcome. All the Celtic races are famous for their hospitality. "They never lock their doors," said one Roman writer. "They invite complete strangers to their feasts and only ask who they are when it is all over."

When you arrive, make sure you follow the Irish custom of saying a prayer of blessing for the house and everyone who lives there.

2 You'll be offered a footbath as soon as you arrive. It's the traditional way to welcome a guest. You'll also be expected to have a bath every night before you go to bed. The Celts are very clean people. They always wash their hair before they go into battle. Many of them manicure their nails and use face

creams made from lanolin (the fat from sheep's wool).

3 Don't expect people to take too much notice of you. The Irish are used to young visitors. They make a habit of fostering each other's children, so you'll be expected to muck in with all the others. And if there is a cattle raid or some other fight, you will probably end up fighting alongside your Celtic foster brothers and sisters.

4 There may also be slaves living with your family. They will be people bought abroad or perhaps captured on raids. The slaves will be doing the heavy work, but otherwise will be reasonably well treated. Some of them may speak English, and will be able to translate between you and your Celtic hosts.

5 Don't be surprised if the mum in the family you are staying with acts like the boss, even if she has a fearsome warrior for a husband. Irish law says that if a husband is less rich than his wife, he is fer fognama (a man of service) and she is the head of the family.

6 The food will be good. Plenty of milk, fish and meat, especially as you will be there in summer time. (In winter the cows give less milk, and animals are not killed for food because they will have babies in the spring.) Veg is mainly seaweed and something called "fat-hen" which is a bit like cabbage. Try the honey cakes and the mead – a drink made from fermented honey. Everyone drinks it from the same bowl, which is passed around the table.

7 There won't be any TV or video games, but the Irish Celts love to play chess and other board games. So improve your chess before you go. Or, you can sit back by the peat fire and listen to one of the storytellers, or bards. Often these guys play the harp and sing their stories. They're well worth listening to.

8 Girls can expect to be taught to spin, which means turning the wool from sheep, or the flax of the linen plant, into thread so that it can be made into clothes. You'll sit at a little spinning wheel to do this, and turn the wheel with a foot pedal, while your hands are busy turning the wool into thread.

9 If you ask, you can probably try your hand at dyeing and weaving as well. Irish tweed and linen are the finest in the world, and you might like to bring some home with you. Or maybe you might like to buy a brooch or "torc" (neck-band). Look out for the special Celtic knot effect.

10 While you are staying with "your" family, behave yourself! There are no policemen where you're going. Instead each family polices its own members, and you will be the responsibility of the family while you're staying with them. If you get into trouble, they will punish you – otherwise, other people will take it out on them.

If you get a chance, go and watch one of the Druid "law-courts." Everyone takes their disputes to the Druids, and when you see how they decide whether somebody is telling the truth, you might be glad to come home again. One way is to heat water to boiling in a cauldron made of gold and silver. Then the accused person dips his hand in. If he is innocent, his hand is not burned. So, don't get yourself accused of lying if you can possibly help it.

WHAT THEY SAID ...

Three things that are always in a decent man's house: beer, a bath, a good fire.
Three sounds of plenty: the lowing of a cow in milk, the noise of a smithy, the sound of the plough.
Three slender things which support the world: the squirt of milk into a bucket, a new shoot of corn coming through the earth, the thread spinning from a woman's hand.

The Triads of Ireland,
old Irish poem

Legend 8: Dermot and Grania

One of the greatest Irish love-stories is that of Dermot and Grania. Grania was a young princess when the all-powerful Finn MacCool decided he wanted to marry her. And Dermot was one of Finn's most trusted warriors, as we saw in Top Ten Legend seven. Finn was not pleased when they ran away together. He chased them all over Ireland. Now, in Top Ten Legend eight, an interviewer from the mag *Wind and Mist*, the Celtic celebrity news-and-pictures paper, tracks them down to a secret location, somewhere in Ireland, for an exclusive interview.

Love on the run

We visit Dermot and Grania – Ireland's most glamorous couple – in their latest home.

She has been called the most beautiful woman in all Ireland. He is known for his dark good looks and the magic mole on his brow which makes every woman fall in love with him. She is the daughter of Cormac, King of Ireland. He is the son of Angus, god of love. They are deeply in love. They are also in exile – on the run from Finn MacCool, lord of the Fenians, who was betrothed to marry Grania himself and has vowed to kill Dermot. We went to visit them at their new – temporary – home. So frightened were they that the location would be recognized that they asked our photographer not to take any pictures of the outside of their dwelling. All they would allow us to say was that it was near a rowan tree. Grania has made the humble dwelling very homely, but there is no disguising the fact that they have no furniture and very few possessions.

Interviewer: Grania, let me start with you first. You are the daughter of a king. You had the chance to marry Finn MacCool, lord of the Fenians. Yet here you are in hiding? Why did you do it?

Grania: I was in love. Besides, there was never any question of my marrying Finn. He is an old man. When he asked me I told him. I said, "What would I want with a grizzled old man like you? It would make more sense to marry me off to your son, Oisin."

Interviewer: Did you want to marry Oisin?

Grania: No. I was already in love with Dermot.

Interviewer: Was this because you caught sight of his love-spot?

Grania: I think it was. Although even before I saw it, I thought he was the most handsome man I had ever seen.

Interviewer: Now you're wearing a metal band around your brow, Dermot. Is that something you do all the time?

Dermot: Yes. I keep the love-spot covered. Grania insists on it!

Grania: You kept it covered long before you met me!

Interviewer: This love-spot was a gift from your father, wasn't it? It makes any woman who sees it weak with love for you?

Dermot: Yes. That's unfortunately the case.

Interviewer: Unfortunately?! So you don't like women falling in love with you?

Dermot: Not really. It's embarrassing. I can't love them all.

Interviewer: How did Grania manage to glimpse your love-spot? Did you leave your band off deliberately that day?

Dermot: No. I was at King Cormac's palace along with Finn and the rest of the Fenians. I was left outside on guard when Finn went into the palace of Tara to speak to Cormac about marrying his daughter.

Grania: And I was watching from the windows. And I thought, who is that beautiful boy?

Dermot: And the day was hot, and I thought I was alone. I took off my helmet.

Grania: And I brought him a glass of water.

Interviewer: And saw the love-spot?

Grania: Yes. And that was that. Love at first sight!

Interviewer: What about you, Dermot? Were you in love with Grania?

Dermot: Not to start off with.

Grania: He had to be persuaded.

Dermot: Only because I knew Finn wanted you. And Finn was my lord. I owed him my loyalty.

Grania: But I was desperate. I knew my father wanted me to marry Finn – and that Finn wanted me to marry Finn. And I knew I wasn't going to.

Interviewer: The press at the time reported that you drugged everyone at the engagement party.

Grania: You make me sound dreadful. I'll tell you what happened. Finn gave a great banquet to celebrate his betrothal. And I'm thinking – hang on here, *I'm* the one who's getting married. Don't I have a say? I looked across the table at Finn. Now he's been a great fellow in his day, but for a girl my age – I was only fifteen – let's face it, it would have been like marrying my grandfather.

And then I looked across at Dermot with his beautiful dark curly hair, and his fine legs, and I thought, that's the man for me. So I slipped out and with one of my maidservants, I spiced a great quantity of mead with a drug I knew about from a Druid. And then I came back into the feast, and offered this drink as my special contribution to the feast.

Dermot: She made sure I didn't get any of the potion, though.

Grania: Yes. There was one pitcher that was not drugged, and I poured Dermot's drink from that. So when the rest of them were all flat out and snoring, young Dermot here was the only one still upright. That's when I told him my feelings.

Interviewer: What did you say, Dermot? Were you flattered?

Dermot: Yes, of course.

Grania: No you weren't. You were terrified.

Dermot: Well, er, I –

Grania: You were *terrified.*

Dermot: Only because, as I said before, it was an act of disloyalty to Finn.

Interviewer: You obviously changed your mind.

Dermot: Well. Not really. What happened was, she put a *geas* on me. You know what that means? It means the poor man is powerless. He has to do what the woman wants.

Grania: Absolute rubbish, Dermot. Now that's what men always say. Anything to avoid taking responsibility.

Dermot: She put a *geas* on me. She said I had to run away with her that night. And I said, "How can I come with you, the gates are barred?" And she said, "You can leave by the women's gate." Apparently there was some little wicker gate that was always left unlocked for the women. And I said, "There is no way I am leaving by the women's gate."

Grania: And I said, "Well, you're a Fenian. The Fenians are supposed to be able to vault any wall. I'll go out by the women's gate, and you vault the palace wall."

Interviewer: So that's what happened?

Dermot: That's what happened. By dawn we were long gone.

Grania: We had to be. We knew Finn. We knew he would be after us with every man and horse and hound that he had.

Interviewer: Now I know you had a very difficult time after that for many years.

Dermot: Yes. It's been hard. We daren't stop long anywhere. If we eat in a place, we don't stop there to sleep. If we sleep in a place, we're up long before the dawn. For years we've slept in caves and trees and under rocks.

Interviewer: You gave up everything for love. Was it worth it?

Grania: Oh, it's been worth every second of hardship.

Dermot: It's worth it. I've grown to love Grania more each day.

Interviewer: And you've managed to keep one step ahead of Finn?

Dermot: Aye, but there've been some mighty close shaves. My goodness.

Interviewer: Would you like to tell us about one of those?

Grania: Well, I think the worst time was when we were hiding in a rowan tree. In a house that had belonged to a giant. And Finn got wind that we were there, and came and sat beneath the tree.

Dermot: Playing chess with my best friend Oisin.

Grania: And Dermot couldn't bear to see Oisin lose, so he started dropping berries down on the chess board. And Finn looked up into the branches of the tree and

saw the pair of us looking down at him through the leaves.

Interviewer: How terrifying! What did you do?

Grania: Well. Dermot's dad, Angus, had always promised to hide us in a magic mist, if ever we needed it. But Dermot would never ask for that, not for himself. He's always said it would be cowardly to disappear by magic like that. But this was serious, so he asked Angus to take care of me. And so I disappeared into a mist and Angus spirited me away to safety.

Interviewer: But what about you, Dermot? What did you do?

Grania: I'll tell you what he did. He ran along the longest branch of the rowan tree, over the heads of Finn and all his men, and took a flying leap over the river, and then he legged it. Mile after mile he ran, over mountain and bog. There was no one could keep up with him. He's such a warrior. There's no one to touch him.

Interviewer: You're obviously still deeply in love with each other.

Dermot: Yes. Well, we've been through so much together. And then there's the child. She was born while we were on the run.

Interviewer: But now you're seeking a reconciliation with Finn?

Grania: Yes. It's crazy that we're still in exile after all these years.

Dermot: And we're not getting any younger ourselves. It's hard work, moving from place to place, never able to settle down.

Grania: Besides, it's time our daughter came to court. She shouldn't be camping in caves and disused houses. She's the grand-daughter of a god and king after all.

Interviewer: Do you think it's likely Finn will forgive you?

Dermot: Well, I don't want to say anything that might prejudice the issue.

Grania: There are signs. There are signs. My father says he's mellowed a little. And of course, Oisin and all Dermot's friends have always said Finn was out of order.

Dermot: Grania. . .

Grania: What?

Dermot: You don't know that. They've never said that.

Grania: I know what my ladies tell me.

Interviewer: You're obviously no less headstrong now than you were as a young woman, Grania.

Grania: No. Why should I be? I'm tougher now than I was when I was a young woman. And guess who's responsible for that? Finn MacCool.

Interviewer: Well, we'll have to leave it there. But

thank you both very much. Let's hope you'll soon be out of exile and free to appear at court.

After giving this interview Dermot and Grania and Finn made up their quarrel, and Dermot and Grania came out of hiding. Unfortunately Dermot met with a terrible accident not long afterwards, when he was killed by a poisonous boar. Six weeks after his death, Grania invited *Wind and Mist* back to speak to her.

Interviewer: It seems a terrible irony that Dermot should have met with such a horrible accident so soon after being forgiven by Finn.

Grania: He was not forgiven by Finn. Finn only pretended to forgive him. He ordered Dermot to kill that boar knowing that he would not survive.

Interviewer: He did kill the boar, though?

Grania: Of course he did. There's no way Dermot would fail to kill a boar.

Interviewer: So perhaps you could just explain how it

was that Dermot met his death.

Grania: He died because Finn MacCool ordered him to walk barefoot on the dead boar's back.

Interviewer: It seems a strange thing to do.

Grania: It is a strange thing. But there was method in Finn's madness. He knew that the boar's bristles were poisonous. They penetrated poor Dermot's feet.

Interviewer: It's obviously very distressing for you to speak about this.

Grania: Yes. But I want to speak. I want everyone to know Finn MacCool for what he is. Because he could have saved Dermot. He has the power of healing in his thumb. And when Dermot lay dying, he begged Finn to bring him water. And Finn played at bringing it. He went and fetched water in his cupped hands. And then as he approached Dermot, he let the water run though his hands on to the ground. Can you imagine? To play with a dying man!

Interviewer: In fact, a spokesman for Finn has said that the reason for this behaviour is that Finn was in great conflict. That when he thought of Dermot, the brave warrior, he longed to save him. And when he remembered that he had stolen you, his young bride, he felt great hatred and let the water slip through his fingers.

Grania: You can believe that if you like. I think he was simply taunting poor Dermot.

Interviewer: Is it true that Finn has sent a proposal of marriage to you?

Grania: He has ordered me to marry him, if that is what you mean.

Interviewer: Are you going to?

Grania: What do you think? No I am not. I loved Dermot. I will love him till my dying day. There will never be anyone else for me. As for marrying my husband's murderer, the man who's persecuted us these fifteen years – forget it.

Grania did marry Finn in the end. Probably she had to – he was the chief of the Fenians after all. But she never forgot Dermot. He was the one she loved in her heart till the end of her life.

Top Facts 8: At home with the Celts

Ever wanted to recreate the Celtic Look in your own home? Today's featured interior is the barely-furnished Celtic broch or barn. Here are ten top tips for how to achieve the Celtic look.

1 First build yourself a broch – a circular building made of stone. They come in various sizes, and some of them have several rooms with connecting corridors. For a big broch you will need several thousand large round stones. Put the biggest ones at the bottom, and the smaller ones higher up. The floor is beaten earth, which makes it easy to keep clean because dirt and mud just don't show! Put rushes on the floor mixed with sweet herbs and change them every few days.

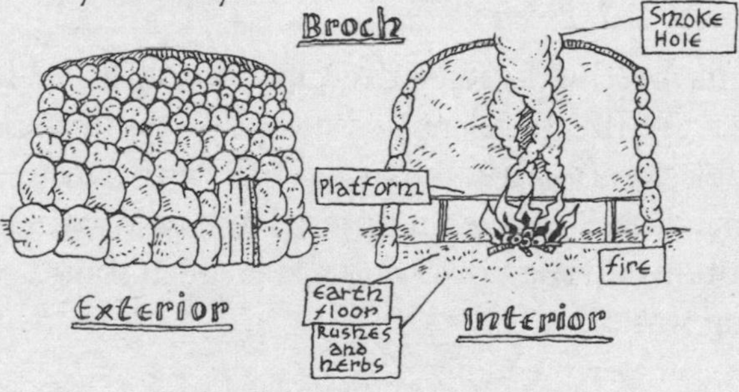

Heat your broch with a peat fire in the central room. You can cook and roast meat on this. You don't need a chimney – just leave a hole in the roof and the smoke will find its way out.

For sleeping, build a wooden platform for the family – that way you can keep your animals downstairs safe from sheep and cattle thieves.

2 Want a banqueting hall for special occasions? You can make a fantastic hall by cutting wands from hazel and willow trees. Weave the willow and hazel wands together to make wattle walls. Then fill all the spaces in the wattle with moss and mud. Last, seal them with clay – then you can get going with the paintbrush. Remember, if you want it to look authentic, you should use only natural dyes made from dandelions and onion skins. For the roof you will need thatch, supported by stronger beams – oak is best.

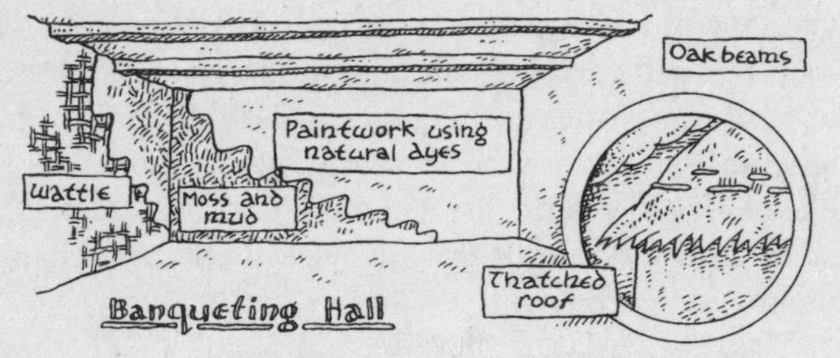

3 Or maybe you'd prefer the Otherworld look? In that case, forget the hazel and the mud – build yourself a house of silver wattle and thatch it with white swan's feathers. Build it over a spring, and you can have a fountain inside the house and the magical sound of fresh running water.

4 Don't think you have to do without all mod cons. You can keep the Celtic look and still have a sauna. You build a little beehive out of stones. Next put a good thick layer of grassy turf for the roof. Inside you need a tub of water – a big stone boulder hollowed out is ideal. Light a big fire outside the sauna – preferably a little higher up the hill. Heat stones in the fire until they are red hot, then roll them down and into the trough of water in the sauna. You'd be surprised how hot the water will get – boiling, in fact. Soon you'll have some great steam going – perfect for those aching muscles when you get home from hunting or fighting.

5 Don't forget the garden. Although the big circles of standing stones were built long before the Irish Celts, they liked to remember the ancestors, and so should you. Why not build something small and manageable like a dolmen or burial mound? Dolmens consist of about three standing stones with a big stone or capstone lying across them to form a little room. They're often called the "beds of Dermot and Grainne". Always remember that it's a good idea to enlist the help of the Druids in siting these stones – it's important that they are correctly lined up with the stars, though no one knows quite why.

6 Nail a few human skulls up on the doors and battlements. No Celtic castle is complete without plenty of heads. You get them from the necks of your enemies. Slice them off before or after you've killed them, it doesn't much matter which, and then stick them up on spears or hang them on doors. This is not merely decorative. Every good Celt knows that the head contains the soul and power of a man – so by hanging his head on your castle you're making sure his power works for you, not against you. And if for some reason you don't have quite enough of the real thing, remember, you can always carve a few severed heads on your gateposts and walls.

7 Come Samhain, don't forget to light reed candles inside the skulls. This scares any Otherworld types who might have been allied to your man when he was alive – not to mention his mortal allies. They look very picturesque too, particularly when the flesh has rotted away and yellow light is shining out of the holes where eyes, nose and mouth used to be. For squeamish types, or those who've had a poor crop of heads this year, a large turnip can be dug out and carved to look like a human head. From a distance it is just as effective. Maybe you already do this without knowing it's an old Celtic custom?

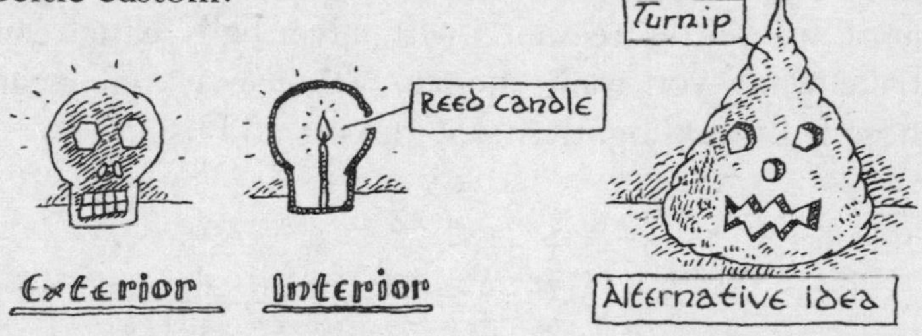

8 Invest in a good cauldron. No Celtic home is without one. These come in all varieties, from simple cooking pots, to huge, silver and gold cauldrons, carved with gods and animals. If you're buying second-hand, and you want something which will increase in value, try to find one by Giobniu (the divine blacksmith) or better still by Credne, the god who designed all the earliest Irish metalwork. These are very special.

9 For the table you might like some tankards made of yew, covered with thin bronze sheeting. Look out for the new decorative handles, also in bronze, featuring the "Celtic knot".

10 Do you find that your family never listens when you speak? What you need is a *crann tamhail*, as used by Irish kings. It's a little tree hung with silver bells, which you shake when you want silence. When everyone hears those bells tinkling, they stop talking and listen.

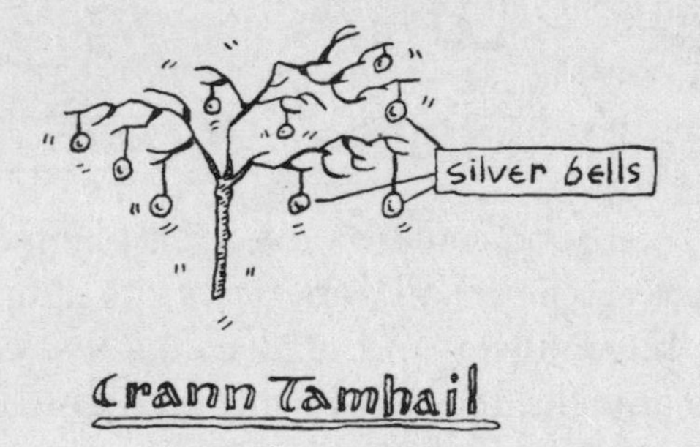

Crann Tamhail

Legend 9: Oisin in the Otherworld

With Top Ten Legend number nine, the day of the great, larger-than-life Irish heroes is nearly over. When you get to the end, you'll see why. Ireland was changing. New beliefs and ways of doing things were on the way. Yet – according to the storytellers – the changes weren't all for the better. They mourned the Good Old Days. They even said the new breed of men who lived in Ireland were tiny pygmies compared to the heroes of old.

Finn's son, Oisin, was one of those who lived long enough to see the changes – and he managed that by disappearing to the Otherworld.

So here – coming in as Top Ten Celtic Legend number nine – is Oisin's story. It's another tale of love, with a beguiling lady from the Otherworld, and it's been made into a blockbuster movie for the wide screen. Here it's reviewed by popular Teen Mag, *Dream On*.

DREAM ON...
Celtic Blockbuster Movie Review

Stranded in Paradise

Starring Leonardo Mac Caprio as Oisin, Arianrhod Winslett as Niav and Conal Connery as Finn MacCool.

THE STORY

1. First we meet our hero Oisin, son of Finn MacCool. He's out hunting one cold still winter's morning with his Dad when they lose their way and find themselves beside Loch Lene. No one in sight – then Finn hears a horse with silver shoes approaching!

2. Next the lovely Niav of the Golden Hair (Arianrhod Winslett) comes riding across the surface of the lake. She tells Finn she has come to ask for something that is his but which he doesn't possess. It's Oisin, of course. She's fallen for that tuft of deer's hair on his brow and she wants to take him back to her kingdom beyond the sea.

3. As Niav talks about the Otherworld, all the Fenians fall asleep except for Oisin. Niav promises him a hundred horses that can outrun the wind, and a hundred hounds who can outrun the horses. If that weren't temptation enough she also offers a hundred huntsmen and a hundred maidens who will sing him to sleep in their arms. Oisin cannot resist. (Could you?) She takes him on her horse and rides away in a mist of spray and sunlight.

4 Meanwhile Finn and his men have woken up and start looking for Oisin. They ask the local farmers and fishermen but no one has seen him.

5 Oisin arrives in the Land of Youth. As he and Niav ride ashore among smiling crowds of people, Niav points out the orchards and fruit bushes as far as the eye can see. Not to mention meadows of flowers, fields of ripe grain, sun shining out of a clear blue sky. Then there are the hills where people farm dreams and the valleys where they live in silence. And of course, time doesn't exist. Niav gives him the good news and the bad: the minute he puts his foot on the ground he will become Lord of the Land of Youth, but he will never be able to go home.

6. Oisin decides to stay. He jumps down from the horse – and undergoes a sudden change! His clothes turn from rough woollen material to fine silk, his skin darkens, his frown lines fall away, and his hair turns to gold.

Does Oisin live happily ever after? You'll have to watch the movie to find out!!

Verdict: if you like your movies soft-focus and romantic, this is the film for you. As well as great performances from the young stars, the landscape is a knockout. But there is a deeper message here too – about how you can never turn back. 7 out of 10. ★★★★★★★

The Sequel

Stranded in Paradise was such a massive success at the box office, that the film company has already produced a sequel. Here Dream On previews that second film.

Return from Paradise

Starring Leonardo Mac Caprio as Oisin, Arianrhod Winslett as Niav and Liam MacNeeson as Saint Patrick

1. It's ten years on and our Oisin is bored with happiness, smiling people and endless summer fruit. Niav knows it and asks him if he'd like to go home on a visit.

2. Oisin needs no second invite. He's on his way, riding over the sea, Niav's magic horse kicking up spray as they go.

3. Back in Ireland the weather is dreary and all Oisin can see are very small men digging the land. He asks them where he can find his father, but the only word they understand is Finn MacCool.

4. The men show Oisin a ruin and tell him this was Finn's castle. At last Oisin understands that centuries have passed since he went away.

5. Suddenly Niav's horse rears up. Oisin falls to the ground and in that moment he ages hundreds of years. His clothes rot, his hair turns to powder, his skin wrinkles and his teeth fall out. This is Leo Mac Caprio as you've never seen him before!

6. The small men pick up the ancient Oisin and take him to meet St Patrick. He offers to baptize Oisin. Oisin asks what would be the point. St Patrick tells him he would go to paradise. When he describes it, Oisin thinks it sounds a lot like the Otherworld, pretty good **and** bad really!

7. Oisin tells Patrick he wants to meet his father. Will Finn be in paradise? Patrick says he won't be if Finn was not baptized. At this the ancient Oisin gets angry and tells Patrick his God is mean. Patrick calms Oisin down and asks him about Finn. How did the ancient Celts cope with the misery of life when they had no Jesus Christ to believe in?

8. Meanwhile, in an underground cave, the huge Finn and his huge men and huge horses stir at the sound of their names. They are not dead, but sleeping, awaiting the day when they will be needed to come and fight for Ireland once more. As Oisin tells Patrick about his father, Finn and his men come to life and relive their old adventures once more.

Verdict: a much more sombre movie than Stranded. The love story's over, Leo's a crumbly, and Patrick's a pretty cold fish. Things look as if they will cheer up when Finn comes to life, but it doesn't alter the fact that the superheroes are dead and gone. 4 out of 10. ★★★★

Top Facts 9: Celtic fashion, fact and fiction

On Thursday, all the glitziest celebrities of the Celtic world gathered for the annual Fashion Awards. Here's what they wore – and this is just the audience!

1 Manannan Mac Lir wears a long purple fringed coat, with threads of gold running though it. His shoes are white bronze and he carries a silver branch on which grow three golden apples.

2 Cuchulain arrives in his chariot wearing a crimson five-folded tunic, fastened with a gold brooch over a white hooded shirt, and edged with red-and-gold embroidery. This shows off his dark good looks and especially his eyebrows, described as "black as a charred beam" by one of the young girls swooning at the gate. Note the crimson shield with the silver edge carved with animals, and the gold hilt to his sword.

3 The Morrigan, dressed from head to foot in red, to match her flaming hair, as she was on the fateful day she came to offer her love to a Cuchulain too tired to say yes to her. Note the grey spear strapped to her

back, and the way the cloak hangs down over her chariot wheels.

4 Ferdiad, dressed for his battle at the ford with Cuchulain, wears seven layers of silk, leather and stone, covered by an overall of beaten-iron. On his head, he wears a helmet encrusted with jewels, and on his back a huge shield with fifty large knobs around its edge.

5 Etain wears a robe edged with silver, a green silk tunic embroidered with gold and fastened with pins of silver and gold; a purple cloak. Her make-up is by Nature Knows: wild foxglove lipstick, bluc-hyacinth eye-liner, new-fallen-snow panstick.

6 Midir in the costume he wore when he first came to reclaim Etain. The green cloak she talks about in her diary hangs in deep folds, pinned by a huge golden brooch to a scarlet tunic. He has a shield of gold and silver slung over his back by a silver strap. His shoulder-length golden hair is held back from his face by a head-band.

7 Finn MacCool posed for photographers in full battledress: undershirt of fine silk; waxed cotton shirts;

iron chain-mail and decorated golden breastplate. Helmet, inset with gems.

8 The sinister Midac, heir to Lochlann, also in full battledress. He wears a shirt of chain mail, and over it a coat of five colours. His shield is made from a single piece of alder covered with bronze. Note the two deadly spears and the extra-long sword, studded with gems.

9 Oisin in the blue silk tunic and saffron cloak that were his first new clothes in the Land of Eternal Youth. Inset: the rough woollen tunic and hunting cloak in which he arrived in the Otherworld with his bride-to-be.

10 An unknown priestess, dressed in traditional Druid garb – a long white dress, a bronze belt and bare feet.

The stories of old Ireland, however, were first written down by scribes in the Middle Ages. So, vivid as these descriptions are, they tell us more about fashion in medieval Ireland than they do about the time of the Celts. Here's what we *do* know about Celtic fashion.

1 The medieval writers were right in one thing. Celts loved bright clothes. According to Diodorus Siculus, a Roman who wrote a World History in the first century BC: "*They wear amazing clothes; tunics dyed in every colour. . . They pin striped cloaks on top of thick cloth in winter and light material in summer, decorated with small, densely packed, multi-coloured squares.*"
Sounds like an early version of tartan.

2 The Celts were one of the first peoples to invent trousers or breeches. Horsemen and charioteers wore leather breeches with straps crossing under the foot of each leg to prevent their riding up the calf. In fact, the word "breeches" is one of the few Gaelic words which has entered the English language.

3 Never mind what the storyteller tells us about Finn MacCool in full battle-dress. He was a general. Full battle-dress for ordinary Irish Celts was a helmet and a coat of war-paint – or woad (a blue dye from a plant). Warriors liked to wear as little as possible when they fought because that way they could move faster. Also they didn't want their clothes to get messed up. They painted their bodies, not just to make themselves look more frightening, but because woad is antiseptic.

4 Helmets, along with shields and sword handles, were pretty special – particularly if you were a prince or a warrior chieftain. They were often bronze, or gilded silver, and they were traced (decorated) with all sorts of intricate designs.

5 Torcs were big collars made of bronze or silver. Many carvings of the gods and heroes show them wearing torcs. The richer and more important you were, the bigger and fancier your torc. Both men and women wore them.

6 Cloaks were a big deal. The longer and fuller the cloak, the more important you were. Five folds meant you were a really big chief, three meant that you were an ordinary foot-soldier.

7 Hair was worn long, and men washed it before going into battle. For big occasions, they bleached their hair with lime, and then put a mix of beeswax, oil and honey on it to make it stand out in spikes like a Mohican.

8 Women often dyed their hair to match their dresses,

whole chunks in different colours which they wore plaited and wound round their heads. Sometimes they plaited silver or gold threads into it as well.

9 Beards and moustaches were neatly trimmed, and finger and toe-nails carefully manicured. And the Celts used face-creams and probably make-up as well. Some people think that young girls wore nothing on their top half when they were inside the house – except body paint.

10 Bracelets, bangles and earrings were all the rage. The Celts loved jewellery – anything that sparkled in fact. Here's Strabo, another Roman, writing about them in 64 BC: "*They wear a lot of gold. They put golden collars around their necks and bracelets on their arms and wrists, while dignitaries wear dyed or stained clothing that is spangled with gold.*"

Legend 10: Saint Patrick converts the heathen

It was in the fourth century that Saint Patrick came to Ireland as a Christian missionary. He wasn't the first Christian, nor was he Irish, but he was so famous that Ireland adopted him as her patron saint. What's most surprising about Patrick is that he had such a dreadful introduction to Ireland and the Irish that you would have thought he would never have wanted to set foot in the country again. Perhaps he thought that by bringing news of Jesus Christ to the pagans he would turn them into gentler people. Certainly the coming of Christianity meant the end of the old wild Irish heroes. So now read about Saint Patrick's busy life in Top Ten story number one – as written★ by a monk in the Middle Ages.

★ There were no printing presses in those days, so all books had to be copied by hand. They were often illustrated with beautiful lettering and gold paint. The Irish church had one of the best libraries in the world until Medieval times.

Saint Patrick—His True Story

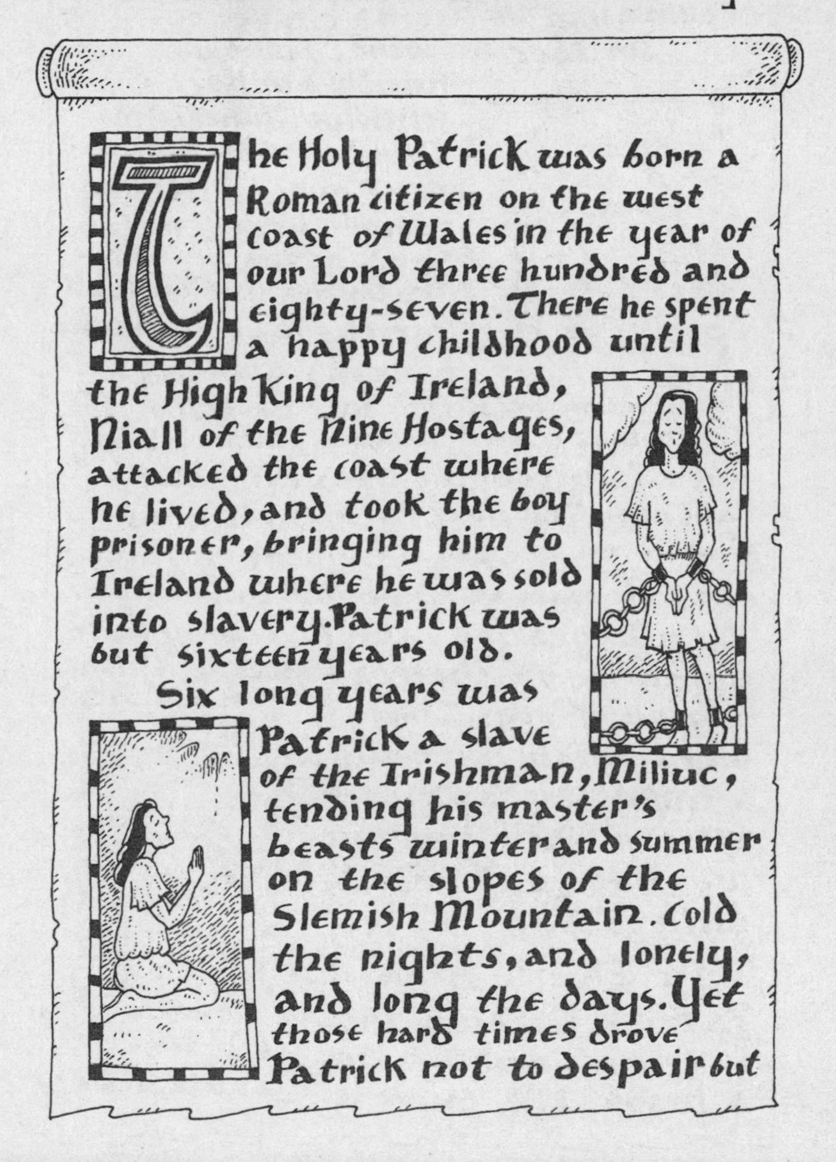

to God. Night and day he prayed. And at this time there came to him a voice, telling him he should escape.

On foot he went, full two hundred miles, to Wicklow, where he found a ship bound for France. Putting ashore in a deserted spot, he and his shipmates set out on foot for the nearest town.

A week's walking in cold wet weather left them weak and hungry, man and dog both. Whereupon cried the sea-captain, "Young Patrick, if your God is so great, let you pray to him that He may send food." Whereupon Patrick prayed, and instantly there appeared on the road before them a herd of pigs. That night did they eat well by a wood fire, and ever after on their journey were they well provided with food.

In France it was that Patrick studied the scriptures and became a monk. And there it was that he slept outside in deepest winter lying beneath a tree heavy with white hoar-frost. And as he slept the frost melted and the tree burst into bloom. And that tree blooms each year in December to this day.

And in France also, the Holy Patrick received a message from his spirit-friend, Victor, who spoke often with him in dreams. And Victor showed him a paper upon which was written "the Voice of the Irish." And Victor told him "The Irish call you. They ask you to come and walk among them once more."

So now did the Holy Patrick return to Ireland. And the year of our Lord was four hundred and thirty-two. And the place he landed was the very place where he had lived as a slave. From there did he go to Emain Macha, setting up a chuch there, which later became first a monastery and

then, by the Grace of Our Lord, a great cathedral.

And in the following year did Patrick perform great miracles and demonstrate to the people the superstition of their old ways. At Easter-tide, which fell that year at the same time as the old Celtic festival which men called Beltane, when all household fires were put out and no man might light them but from the great fire on the Hill of Tara, which men in their superstition called sacred, then did Patrick light the Easter flame in honour of Our Lord.

On seeing this, the old priests [called Druids] were much annoyed, and warned the High King that if Patrick's fire were not soon put out, then it would spread right across Ireland, and the old ways would be gone.

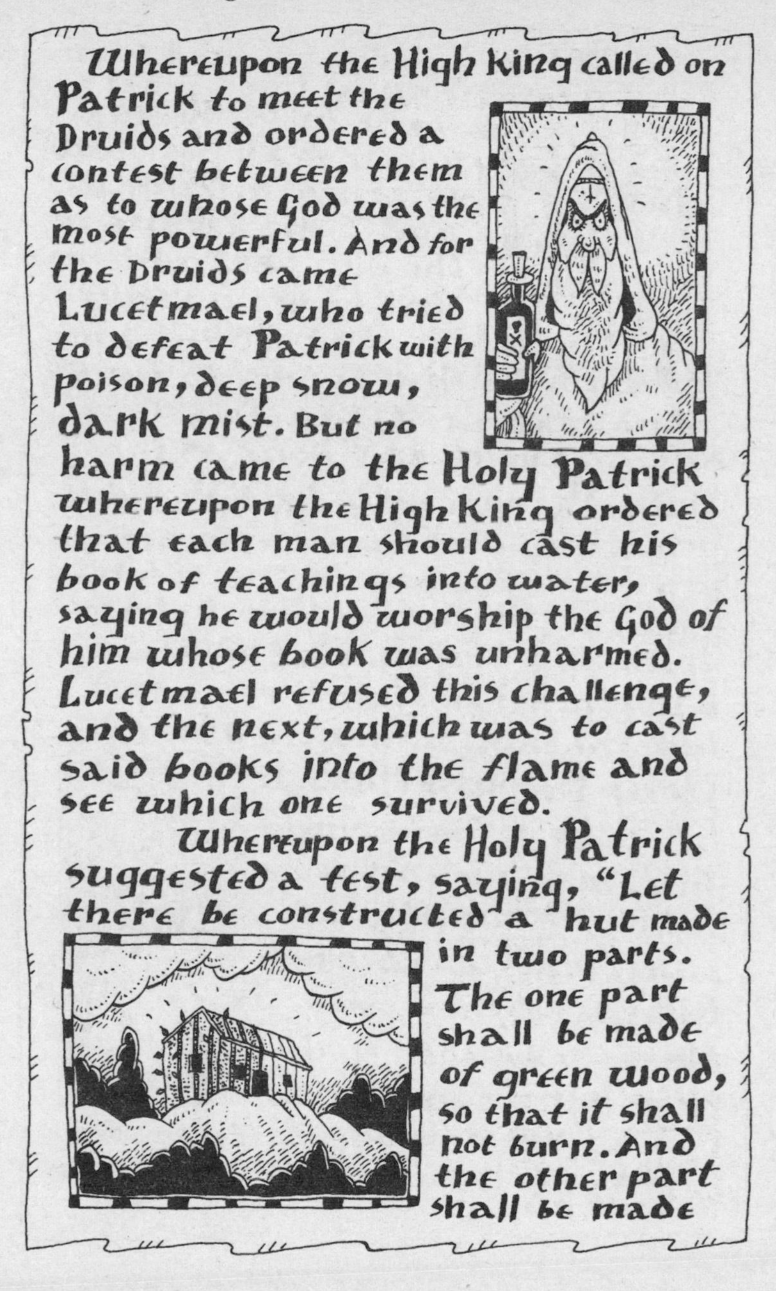
Whereupon the High King called on Patrick to meet the Druids and ordered a contest between them as to whose God was the most powerful. And for the Druids came Lucetmael, who tried to defeat Patrick with poison, deep snow, dark mist. But no harm came to the Holy Patrick whereupon the High King ordered that each man should cast his book of teachings into water, saying he would worship the God of him whose book was unharmed. Lucetmael refused this challenge, and the next, which was to cast said books into the flame and see which one survived.
Whereupon the Holy Patrick suggested a test, saying, "Let there be constructed a hut made in two parts. The one part shall be made of green wood, so that it shall not burn. And the other part shall be made

of dry wood so that it shall burn.

And let Lucetmael stand in the green part which shall not burn wearing my cloak, and I shall stand in the dry part which shall burn wearing his. And let the hut then be put to torch."

And to this test, Lucetmael agreed, and it was done as the Holy Patrick said. And Patrick prayed to our Lord, and then was the hut put to the torch. And the two halves burned, both green and dry wood. And of Lucetmael, nothing remained but the saint's mantle. But the Holy Patrick, though he stood in the burning hut, was unharmed, while the mantle of Lucetmael was burned to ashes. And seeing this, the brother of the High King, Conal Gulban, was baptized, and ever afterwards he was the Holy Patrick's protector in Ireland.

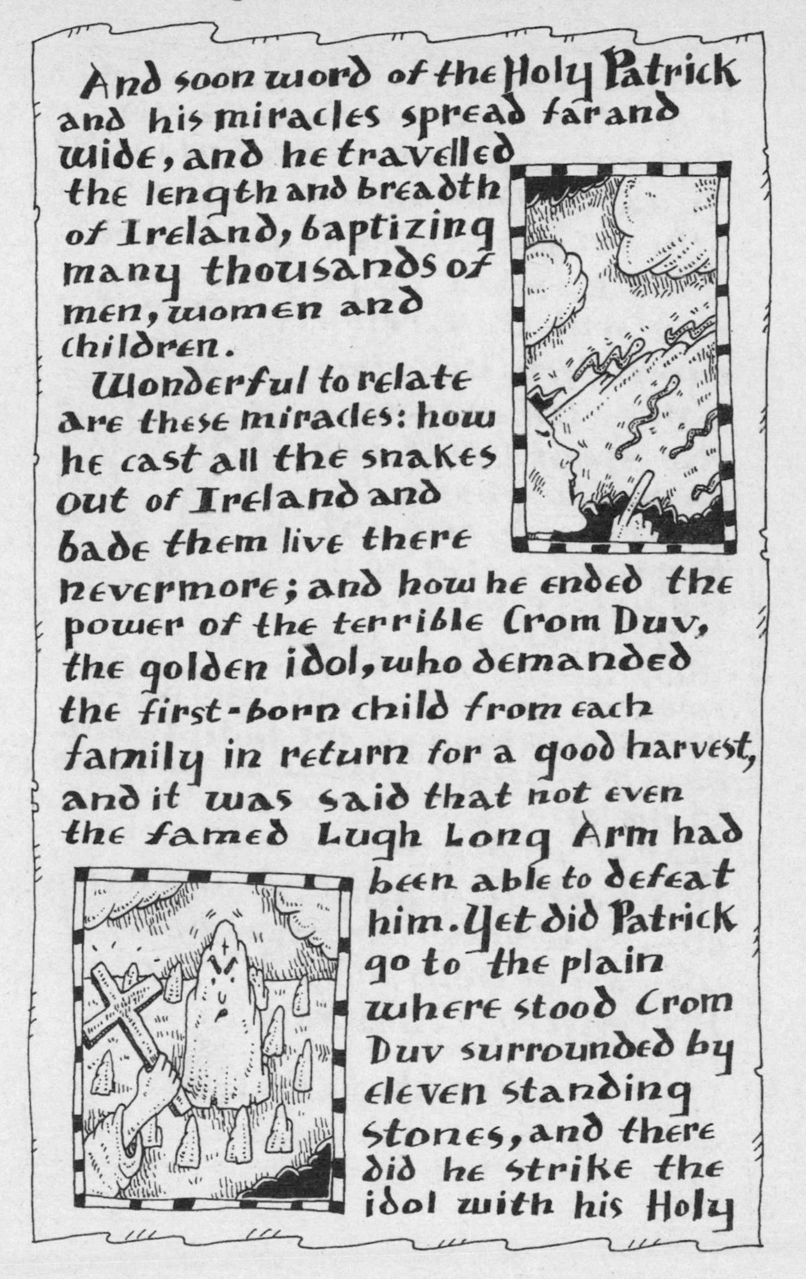

And soon word of the Holy Patrick and his miracles spread far and wide, and he travelled the length and breadth of Ireland, baptizing many thousands of men, women and children.

Wonderful to relate are these miracles: how he cast all the snakes out of Ireland and bade them live there nevermore; and how he ended the power of the terrible Crom Duv, the golden idol, who demanded the first-born child from each family in return for a good harvest, and it was said that not even the famed Lugh Long Arm had been able to defeat him. Yet did Patrick go to the plain where stood Crom Duv surrounded by eleven standing stones, and there did he strike the idol with his Holy

Cross. Whereupon the stone in which lived the power of Crom Duv did keel over, and in the same instant, did the earth open up and swallow the other eleven stones. Whereupon Patrick took a mighty hammer and split the terrible Crom Duv into two halves. Whereupon the spirit left it and rushed helpless to the Otherworld, and the people were free of its evil power for ever.

Wonderful to relate these miracles and many more. But the greatest miracle of all is this: that before the coming of the Holy Patrick there was not a Christian to be found in the land of Ireland, and in the year of his death, in the year of Our Lord four hundred and sixty-one, there was hardly a man, woman or child who did not profess the Christian faith.

Thanks be to God

Top Facts 10: Have you got what it takes?

NEWLY-ESTABLISHED FAST-EXPANDING CHRISTIAN MONASTERY SEEKS RECRUITS.

Connacht Abbey is situated in an isolated spot, minutes from the sea. It is a self-supporting monastery producing all its own food, firewood and wool for clothing and dedicated to the study and preservation of Christian and classical texts.

There are currently vacancies for

Able-bodied novices with experience of agriculture and animal husbandry.
Cooks and vintners.
Scribes (an understanding of Greek, Latin or Syrian an advantage).
Illustrators.
Healers.

Young men showing an aptitude for one of the above can also be trained by the monastery.

There is no pay, but food and lodging is provided. Residential accommodation is provided in the form of individual stone cells (unheated). All meals are also provided and eaten collectively in the refectory
All monks are asked to wear uniform at all times. This is provided and consists of a simple white woollen robe tied with a rope belt, a cloak and a pair of sandals. In addition, all monks will have their hair cut in the traditional Celtic tonsure, and take a vow of obedience to the Abbot of the monastery.
Working hours are 3am–9pm and include prayer, meditation, contemplation, daily labour and church services. Saturday off. No holidays, but a number of Holy Days each year, with special services and celebratory meals.
This is a rewarding life for young men who have no hope of inheriting land.
NO PAGANS NEED APPLY

EPILOGUE

At the same time as Saint Patrick arrived in Ireland, the Roman Empire was falling apart. As the Romans pulled out their troops, the rest of Europe became chaotic. Ireland, which had never been under Roman rule, carried on as usual. In fact, if anything it was more peaceful. Over time the Celtic Church became established in Ireland and soon it was world-famous. Scholars travelled from far and wide to study there.

With the coming of Christianity to Ireland there were no more heroes like Cuchulain and Finn MacCool, and Christian beliefs about Heaven and Hell replaced those about the magical Otherworld. Yet the power of the old stories lived on, sometimes hidden inside the new religion. The Celtic cross, symbol of the Celtic Church, contains a circle, the symbol of Lugh, god of Light. The Dagda's daughter, Brigid, became St Brigid, whose feast day falls on the old Celtic festival of Imbolc, February 1st. And the stories themselves were not forgotten. In fact, it was the monks who helped to preserve them by writing them down.

Since then they've been told over and again. That's the way it is with really powerful stories – they may change, new characters may wander in, but they never die. So the ancient people of Ireland had it right about the power of the storyteller – the heroes and warriors may be dead and gone, but thanks to those early Irish storytellers we still know their names and their deeds today!!